RECLAIMING THE ONE

AIMIE JENNISON

CONTENTS

RECLAIMING THE ONE

MOUNT ROXBY SERIES: BOOK THREE

AIMIE JENNISON

A NOTE FOR
THE READER

This book has been written using UK English and is set in Australia. I apologise if there are words or phrases you do not understand. Please feel free to contact me for further explanation, or to discuss the meaning of a particular phrase or word, via my website www.aimiejennison.com.

DEDICATION

This story is for anyone who feels like they've let *The One* get away.

INVITATION HOME

CAIN - PRESENT DAY

*L*eaving Ruby outside with Theo, Alyssa, and Jared, I enter the house.

Shock hits me to feel such an intense wave of emotion coming from the pack members. I don't know why I'm surprised. Wes was Theo's beta. He was well loved. Of course, the pack are going to be cut up about his death and are going to feel the loss for a long time.

Theo's been on edge ever since I turned up. He doesn't need to be stressing about the past while he's got this hole in his pack to worry about. I came home to see what happened to my little sister, Ruby. She's safe, happy, and mated to a wolf, who I have a hell of a lot of respect for.

Nothing is keeping me here anymore.

Selena's name runs through my mind, but I push it back into the crevice it had been hiding in. I ruined her life a long time ago. When I saw her the day I arrived, she seemed like she was in a good place, looking to the future with her soon-to-be-born baby. I'm not going to spoil that. The best thing for everyone is for me to pack my bag and leave, again.

I make my way upstairs and throw my stuff together. It doesn't take me long because I didn't bring much with me. I'm a metre away from the front door when it pops open. Theo waves Ruby in before him and closes the door.

I can pinpoint the exact moment the wall of sadness hits them: Ruby loses her smile, and Theo takes a deep breath and looks around. Probably looking for someone to comfort. That's when he spots me and my bag. Anger radiates from him.

"My office, now!" he orders, before marching off in the direction of his office.

I'm suddenly transported back in time to when Theo and I had been ordered into Dad's office as kids. We were always getting in trouble. Being as thick as thieves then, we'd both claim to be the one at fault. Dad would then punish us both, saying, "You both deserve it. One of you is lying and one of you did it." Sometimes he'd punish us for nothing, apparently to *"make us stronger."* He was a prick like that. It backfired on him in the end because it did make us stronger. Strong enough to kill him and take over the pack.

Theo is standing with his back to me as I walk in the room. He's staring out the window overlooking the backyard. I close the door and stand in silence watching him, wondering what he's thinking. What he's going to say.

"Were you going to say goodbye? Or were you going to leave another gaping hole? Do you not think the pack has lost enough tonight?" He sounds calm and collected, but I can tell by the fisted hands at his sides that he's pissed.

I join him at the window and sigh as I take in the view of the forest, remembering what it was like to run in those trees. The freedom I could find in there. "I didn't think you needed to be reminded of the past when you have enough of the present to worry about," I say honestly.

He sharply turns his head to look at me. His silence pushes me to say more.

"I know you hate me for what I did, and to be honest, I don't blame you. I don't expect you to forgive me," I admit.

"What is it with my siblings thinking I hate them? I must be one nasty bastard. I don't hate you, Cain. I never did." He rubs at his brows with his fingertips. "You hurt me. You slept with my wife and then you went AWOL. You pissed me off, but you're my brother. I'd never be able to hate you." He sighs. "I fucking love you, you moron," he declares. Catching me off guard, he manages to pull me into a headlock and knuckle my hair.

"Jesus, Theo, what are you? Fucking ten?" We both laugh, and for a second, I forget about the hand the pack was dealt tonight; forget the loss we all feel. We both fall silent, looking to the backyard once again, remembering tonight's events.

"Please stay, Cain. I need a beta who isn't so emotionally affected by the loss of Wes. Someone who can help glue the pack together while they come to terms with it. I need you, Cain."

I glance across at him not believing those words came from his mouth. "What about Ed or Billy? They're both dominant enough to be your beta. Ed seems stronger now he's mated. I haven't been around the pack for over a year. They'll never accept me as their beta."

I left Mount Roxby and became a lone wolf after being caught in bed with Selena, Theo's wife, knowing I wouldn't be accepted as part of the pack any longer. I roamed the country, drifting from pack to pack until I happened to find a mother and child being held captive by a nasty alpha. I managed to help them escape and keep them out of his clutches by moving on when his goons got close. After nine months of being one step ahead of the bad guys, she finally had enough of life on the run and told me who she really was, and I was able to reunite her with her mate, the alpha of the Rossi Pack.

"I'm not the only one who missed you when you left. I think you'll be surprised how many of them will be happy to have you back," he says, as he walks to his desk and pulls out a bottle of whisky and two short glasses. "I know things between the two of us are strained." He pours two glasses and hands me one. "But I trust you with the pack. It's your pack as much as it is mine."

Shock ripples through me at his words, and I down the liquid fire before I speak. "After everything I've done, you still feel like that?"

"I don't know why you did what you did, but I know it wasn't out of malice. That isn't you, never was." He grabs the bottle and tops up our glasses again.

"I need to tell you everything that lead to me sleeping with Selena, and if you still want me to be your beta after that, I'll do it."

He takes a seat on the sofa at the side of the room, places the whisky bottle by his feet, and gestures for me to join him. "Now's as good a time as any."

So I sit down and tell him everything, starting at the very beginning. The day *she* came into my life.

2.

DELECTABLE HONEYSUCKLE

CAIN - EIGHT YEARS AGO

I'm forever running errands for dad's mate, Margie. I hate the woman, and she's made it perfectly clear that the feeling is mutual. I walk out of the corner store with a carton of eggs in my hand when I smell the most alluring scent: honeysuckle. It invades my nostrils and makes my wolf try to jump out of my skin, wanting to roll himself in the delectable fragrance.

I pause in the doorway as I rein in the wolf and look for the female the scent belongs to, knowing she has to be my true mate. No other scent would affect my wolf this way. Excitement rolls through me at the notion. Some wolves can go a lifetime and never find their true mate; and here I am finding mine at the age of nineteen.

My eyes fall on the most beautiful female I've ever laid eyes on. Long dark-blonde hair with golden highlights flows over her shoulders and chest, covering the ample cleavage her low-cut top would be otherwise showing.

The carton of eggs slip through my fingers and I don't even glance down to see them smash on the pavement. I can't take my eyes off the beauty.

At the noise, she glances up from the ground where she'd been focusing as she walked. Her ice-blue eyes lock on mine and she gives me a shy smile.

I smile back, trying not to show the predator I am. Knowing it's my wolf's eyes that are showing, I pull out my shades and slip them over my eyes, hoping she doesn't catch them as he slinks back into his hiding place and they change back to my human eyes. Luckily, my cobalt eyes aren't too different a shade to my wolf's lighter blue ones. I know plenty of people whose eyes are completely different to their wolves'.

"You've made a right mess there, butterfingers." Her silky-smooth voice flows over me. I'm grateful for the shades as my wolf peers out, excited by her voice, yet a little insulted by the nickname.

I take a breath and ground myself, pushing the wolf back once again. I crouch down and try to clear up the mess as best I can, picking up the egg shells and placing them in the soggy carton. "Something caught my eye," I say, unable to think up a witty response with her scent surrounding me.

"I'll get a bucket of water to swill the pavement down. My dad won't be happy if we leave a mess right in the doorway of his shop." She disappears past me and into the building.

I glance in after her and catch sight of an Under New Management sign hanging on the door. I momentarily wonder what happened to Mr Thorpe, but the sight of my blonde beauty heading back towards me with a bucket in one hand and a plastic bag in the other, shoos any thoughts of Mr Thorpe right out of my head. She thrusts the bag in my direction, and I take it, ensuring my fingers brush hers. The contact makes me shiver, and my wolf lets out a content sigh. *Mate.*

"Are you going to step back or do you want the water over you, too?"

Her irritated tone makes me snap out of my trance. What the hell? It's like she's had a personality transplant in the time it took her to get a bucket of water. I stand up while placing the soggy carton containing the broken eggshells into the bag and then see my beauty's arm straining with the weight of the bucket. *That's why she snapped, unaware dick.*

I quickly reach out, taking the bucket's handle. "Here, let me do it. It's my mess after all," I offer, trying to tug the bucket out of her grasp.

She lets go with a shrug. "Give me the bag and I'll stick in the bin." She wiggles her empty hand at me.

Realising I'll be able to direct the water better with two hands, I pass the rubbish over to her. She disappears into the shop once again and I pour the water over the mess of my broken eggs.

Noticing one bucket of water isn't going to be enough to wash away the mess, I head into the shop to look for my beauty or the new manager, her father. "Hello," I call out as I make my way to the counter.

The small balding man, who served me not long ago, pops out a door behind the counter that must lead to a small staff room or office. "Hi, how can I help you?" I hold the bucket up and open my mouth to ask for more water, but recognition crosses his face and he doesn't let me get a word out. "Oh, you're the butterfingers Selena was complaining about. Did one bucket do the job or do you need more water?"

I glance from the bucket to the man before my mouth decides to engage. "It's going to need more water I'm afraid." *Selena.* He called my beauty Selena.

He takes the bucket and goes back through the door shouting over his shoulder, "Grab yourself another carton of eggs while I get us some more water." I stare after him, wondering where Selena's disappeared to and why she hasn't come back, until his words register. My errand for Margie is the reason I came here. If I return without her eggs, I'd be in a world of pain. She's the alpha's mate. My father's mate. If I don't return with her eggs, she'll say I was disobeying an order and demand I be punished for my disobedience. She's an evil bitch. I don't know what my father see's in her.

I walk to the aisle where the eggs are kept and open a carton, making sure to check for cracks and running my hand across them to check they're mobile. If they're stuck to the carton, they're likely to have a crack on the base of them. My mum taught me that before my father tore me away from her and my home.

"That's a neat trick to check for cracks," Selena's soft voice says from behind me.

I jump, clutching the eggs to my chest. The last thing we need is another mess of smashed eggs. How the hell had she crept up on me? My instincts wouldn't normally let that happen. Meeting her has thrown my wolf and me. "Jesus, where did you come from?"

She grins at me, and my heart skips a beat at the sight. I need to see her do that again. Hell, every day. "I didn't realise I looked like a man." She pouts, causing me to open and close my mouth, no doubt doing an awesome impression of a damn goldfish. She laughs, the sound sending shivers down my spine. Good shivers. "Don't hyperventilate. I was only joking. I'm Selena," she says, offering her hand.

I loosen the death grip I have on the eggs and take her hand in my free one. "Cain. Nice to meet you, Selena."

She gives my hand a firm shake and a small voice speaks from behind her. "I'm Maximus. Good to meet you."

I release Selena's hand as she steps aside, giving me a clear view of a boy who can't be much older than seven or eight. His blond mop of hair falling in his ice-blue eyes and his hand held out in my direction, just as Selena's had done a moment ago.

I clear my throat and straighten my shoulders as I take his hand. "It's nice to meet you too, Maximus." His face brightens with an enormous smile and an excited blush travels his cheeks. I release his hand and he looks at his sister as though he has no idea what to do next.

Selena opens her mouth to speak, but before anything escapes, the sound of splashing water takes our attention away from our moment. We all turn and head for the sound of water.

"I would have done that, sir," I say at the same time as Selena speaks.

"Dad. You shouldn't be doing that." She turns her eyes on me, giving me an icy glare. "Why didn't you ask me to refill it? Dad shouldn't be lifting anything."

"I'm sorry, I—" I start before her father cuts me off.

"Let the boy off. He wasn't to know. It's not like I have a sign hanging around my neck—" He swings his arms across his neck. "—saying 'don't let me lift a thing,'" he finishes as he walks through the door and back into the shop, causing us all to stop suddenly, so we don't crash into him.

Selena sighs and gives me an apologetic smile. "He's right. I'm sorry, Cain." Hearing my name roll off her tongue renders me speechless. The only response I can give her is a nod.

"*Daddy…!*" Maximus shouts as he runs into his father, wrapping his arms around his waist, effectively breaking the tension that had risen in the room.

"Hi, Maxie, did you have fun at Jimmy's this afternoon?" their father asks as he leads Max back towards the counter, leaving Selena and me standing in the doorway.

I glance at the eggs in my hand and back towards the counter. "I guess I should go and pay for these."

Selena shakes her head, making her long waves move across her chest drawing my eyes to her cleavage. "No, Dad won't charge you for them. They were broken on our property."

I glance out the door where I had dropped the eggs. "It was my fault and I was out the door. I should pay," I insist wide-eyed, knowing the eggs were all intact when I left the store.

"It will be a waste of your time and breath arguing with my

dad, but go ahead and give it a try," she offers with a wave of her hand in her father's direction.

I bite my lip wondering what to do. She obviously knows her father best, and if she says he won't take any money from me, she's probably right.

"Okay." I pull my wallet out and hand her a five-dollar note. "Here. Will you slip that into the till for me later?"

A broad smile crosses her face, making her eyes light up, and I feel like giving her all the notes in my wallet. "I can do that. Thank you."

"No worries, beautiful." The compliment slips out before I can stop it. I feel my cheeks heat up.

She drops her eyes to her feet as her face flushes. I want nothing more than to pull her into my arms and kiss her to make her blush more.

Walking home from the store, I can't wipe the smile off my face. I've found my true mate.

3.

EXPLAINING THE PAST

CAIN - PRESENT DAY

My eyes come back into focus, the memories of the past fading back to where they belong—in the deep recesses of my mind.

Theo's eyes connect with mine, a frown creasing his brow. "Why didn't you ever tell me? I fucking married her." He runs a hand through his hair. "I married my brother's mate." The pain in his eyes infuriates me. This shouldn't be hurting him. I'm the one who's been separated from my mate for the last eight years.

"Fuck, Theo. Do you not think I wanted to?" Grabbing the bottle at Theo's feet, I fill both our glasses with the amber liquid. "I wanted to tell everyone. To scream it from the fucking rooftops." I take a sip as I pull my anger back. It's not Theo I'm mad at. "That day, when I got back, I'd barely stepped foot in the door when Dad decided I needed to go out of town on pack business. I tried to tell him, but you know Dad, he wouldn't listen to a nineteen-year-old. I was a kid."

"What about when you got back?" Theo runs his finger around the rim of his glass. "I would have listened."

I place my empty glass on the floor at my feet and settle back on the sofa. "By the time I got back into town, you'd been dating her for two months. You were happier than I'd ever seen you. I couldn't take that away from you. Neither of us had been happy since Dad took us away from Mum and Ruby. You'd been away from them longer than I had. You deserved that happiness."

"She is your fucking true mate, Cain. My happiness should never have come into it." The growl in his voice isn't backed up by anger in his wolf's energy.

I shrug. "What can I say? I'm a dick." My words elicit a short laugh from Theo. "It killed me to watch you two together. My wolf wanted to tear you apart. That's why I could never hunt with the pack. I couldn't trust him around you." I rub a hand over my chest, trying to ease the ache that's been there for the last eight years. "I've been torn in two ever since that fucking day."

Theo leans forward on the sofa, placing his head in his hands. "And I just thought you were a moody bastard. I guess that's why you left the pack?" I nod, even though I know he won't see me. "It kind of all makes sense now." He turns to me and places a hand on my knee. "You should have told me. When I found Bel, I knew she was my true mate, but I wasn't able to claim her for a few weeks. So I can only just begin to imagine how hard it must have been for you all those years."

"I fought the attraction as much as I could. Fuck, I dated Chloe on and off over the years, but she knew I would never commit and she started to resent me for it. My wolf just got more and more restless," I say with a sigh, remembering how he felt at the time. Not that he feels any different now. He's constantly pacing inside me, waiting for my defences to drop just enough for him to escape.

"But you slept with her in the end? How the hell did you walk away after that?" Theo asks, clearly curious… and sadly mistaken if he thinks that's the first time I'd slept with her.

"The time you caught us wasn't the only time I slept with her," I admit. The wounded look on his face makes guilt surge through me. "Believe me, I hate myself for that. More than you could imagine."

He nods. "Well then, I guess you should tell me the rest of your story."

Getting to my feet, I pace to the window and look at the forest before taking a deep breath and telling him the rest.

4.
SORROW AND PAIN

year has passed since I first met Selena. I've been successful in avoiding being alone with her, even for a minute, because I know that the first time I do, I won't be able to keep my mouth off hers. I've spent the last twelve months obsessing over how she'll taste and how her soft curves will feel under my hands.

The phone rings in its cradle on the counter, and I pick it up as I flick the switch on the kettle. I was meant to be making coffee. "Wilson residence."

"Mr Wilson?" a grandmotherly voice asks.

"Yes," I answer, even though I know she could easily be after Theo or our dad.

"I'm a nurse at Mount Roxby hospital. I have a Selena Graham here. She has you down as an emergency contact." She pauses, and my breath hitches in my chest. Selena's in the hospital? But before I can say anything aloud, the nurse speaks again. "Now, don't worry. She only has a few superficial cuts and bruises. Unfortunately, I can't say the same for her father and brother. They didn't make it. As you can imagine, she's not handling it very well. We had to sedate her, and I thought it might be good for a familiar face to be here when she wakes up."

I glance at the clock on the wall, my heart racing in my

chest. "I can be there in fifteen minutes. Will she be awake before then?"

"Don't rush. She'll be out for at least another hour. We don't need another accident on the road." She hangs up and I blindly place the phone back in its cradle. My mind races. Selena's lost her brother and father. Theo is all she has left. *Shit!* Theo. He's out of town.

Pulling my mobile out of my pocket, I quickly dial his number.

"Cain. The house is still standing, right?" I can hear the smile in his voice. Every time I call when he's out of town, he answers asking the same thing. He'll never let me forget the time I set fire to the kitchen when Dad left us both in charge.

"Theo, I just had the hospital on the phone. Selena's been in an accident." I rub my sweaty palms on my jeans, swapping the phone from one hand to the other. "She's uninjured," I go on, hoping to ease any panic he may be feeling. "But her father and brother didn't make it. They've sedated her and want a familiar face to be there when she wakes up. They said she'll be out for another hour." I hop from one foot to the other, eager to end this call and make my way to the hospital. I need to see Selena. I need to see she's safe.

"Fuck!" I hear something crunch in the background, leaving me thinking he's punched something, most probably a wall. "There's no way I can get home in time. Even if I manage to get on the next flight, it's a four-hour trip, and that's providing I don't have a stopover in Adelaide or Melbourne. She doesn't really have any friends I can call to go, and none of the pack girls like her."

"I'll go," I offer, planning on going anyway. Nothing's going to stop me.

"Thanks, bro. Take care of her until I get there. I'll text you my flight details as soon as I know them." He hangs up and I stare at the phone for a minute before slipping it back in my pocket and making my way to my car, not bothering to lock the door behind me. It's the pack house, and there's always someone coming and going. It's pointless locking a door when werewolves with supernatural strength are involved. Handles break too easily.

***

The nurse leads me through the ward and stops in front of a blue door. "Selena's in here." She glances down at her watch. "I'll be back before she wakes up. You've got time to go grab a coffee if you like?"

I shake my head. "No. I'd like to sit with her if that's okay?"

"Of course, dear. She's a lucky girl to have a partner like you." She gives me a smile and dashes off towards the nurses' station before I can correct her.

I stare at the door and can't help but think all my avoidance techniques will have been for nothing the second I set foot into the room beyond. Reaching out, I open the door. I pause in the doorway as I'm overwhelmed by Selena's honeysuckle scent.

The sight of her laid out on the bed has me moving, and I'm standing beside her in a second. I stroke her long locks with my hand. "My beauty…," I whisper as I allow my eyes to roam over her, checking for injuries. She has a cut on her forehead and another on her right cheekbone.

She lets out a small moan and my hand freezes on her head, not wanting to be the cause of any pain. "Shh… you're okay, Selena." I try to comfort her, not knowing if she can hear me.

Her eyes flicker open and shut again. "C…" She clears her throat. "Cain?"

"Yes. It's me, beautiful." The term of endearment leaves my mouth without even thinking about it. "Theo's trying to get a flight back from Perth. I'll stay with you until he gets back, if that's okay?"

"Dad? Maxie?" Her question hangs in the air, leaving me to wonder how the hell to break the news. Her eyes pop open and lock onto mine before she lets out a scream, no doubt seeing the answer in my eyes.

"I'm sorry…. We're going to look after you," I state, referring to my wolf and I, before quickly correcting myself. "Theo will look after you, okay? You won't be alone."

She falls into silent sobs, and sitting on the edge of the bed, I gently pull her into my arms, making sure not to hurt any injuries I can't see.

The door opens and the same nurse from earlier walks in. She lets out a surprised noise. "Oh, Miss Graham, you're awake. How are we feeling?"

Selena's sobs become louder as she cries into my chest.

"She's a little upset." I state the obvious.

"Understandably so," the nurse says, before walking over and holding a piece of paper out towards me. I reach for it with the hand that had been stroking large circles on Selena's back. "Selena's discharge papers," she explains.

"She doesn't need to stay… be observed?" I ask, disliking the idea of her not being near medical help if she may need it. The pack has our own doctors and nurses, but they specialise in weres, not humans. And Selena knows nothing about the pack or werewolves.

"She's been thoroughly checked over and has no injuries that require observation."

My wolf growls at the thought of her being checked over. Nobody but us should be checking her over. I quickly remind him that she's Theo's, not ours. In my mind's eye, he bares his teeth at me in a snarl, not happy with that prospect either.

Selena lifts her head and looks up at me with her red-rimmed eyes. "I can't go home. I don't want to be there without them…. I… I…."

I squeeze her gently. "It's okay, beautiful. I'll take you to my home."

The gratitude in her teary eyes cuts into me. "Thank you."

The drive home is quiet, but I hold her hand in mine the whole way, indicators be damned.

Once in the house, I lead her into the lounge as I call out. "Anyone home?" Receiving no reply and knowing any werewolf who may be here would have heard me regardless of what room they may be in, I come to the conclusion that we're home alone.

I focus my attention to Selena. "Here, beautiful. Sit down." I guide her down onto the sofa. Her dazed expression has me worried the doctors may have missed a concussion or something.

Leaving her on the sofa, I head into the kitchen to make her a hot chocolate. My phone vibrates in my pocket and I quickly pull it out. The caller ID telling me who it is. "Theo. When will you be in?"

"I won't be landing until four in the morning. By the time I make it through the traffic, it will be close to six when I get in. How's she doing?"

Opening the door, I peek out and see Selena staring into space, exactly where I'd left her. "She's... honestly, I have no idea. She seems overwhelmed and spaced out. I'm just making her a hot chocolate. I figure the sugar might help with the shock." I go back to mixing the hot chocolate.

"Thanks for looking out for her, Cain. What would I do without you?"

Guilt surges through me at his words. He'd be so much better off with me away from them both, because sooner or later, if I don't tear him to shreds, I'll be ravaging her. Damn the consequences.

"I'm sure you'd manage just fine. Hell, you'd be safer

without me ar—" I pause midsentence, realising I've spoken aloud and said too much.

"What the fuck do you mean by that?" The anger in Theo's voice is clear as a bell down the line.

"I'm going to have to go. Selena's crying," I lie, knowing he won't sense it over the phone.

He huffs. "I'm not going to forget about this. We'll pick this up later." He hangs up, and I know Theo well enough to believe what he says. I'll have to have the conversation with him eventually. Hopefully he'll be distracted with Selena long enough for me to come up with something that he won't sniff out as bullshit.

Grabbing the two mugs off the side, I head back into the lounge. I place a mug on the coffee table and crouch before Selena with the other. "Selena?" Placing a hand on her knee, I squeeze it gently, hoping to catch her attention more since my words got nothing. "Selena, I've got a hot chocolate for you here."

Her eyes drop down to the cup I'm holding and then up to my eyes, slowly seeming to focus. She smiles and my heart skips a beat. "Thanks." She reaches out with both hands and takes the mug from my one-handed hold.

I begrudgingly remove my hand from her knee and grab my mug off the coffee table as I take a seat beside her. "Do you want me to turn the TV on?" I reach for the remote in anticipation of her answer, not at all liking the silence between us. It makes me want to tell her things. Things I should never tell her.

I catch sight of her head shaking. "No, I can't bear to watch happy families at the minute." I pull my hand back without picking up the remote and sip my hot chocolate. I watch out the corner of my eye as Selena blows gently over hers.

"Tell me something… anything. Anything that will distract

me from thinking about…." She doesn't need to say the words. I know she means her family.

My wolf jumps forward wanting to comfort her. "I fell in love with you the first time I laid eyes on you." The words fall out of my mouth, catching me by surprise and her too, if her sharp turn of the head, wide eyes, and slack jaw are anything to go by.

I never meant to tell her that. *Ever.* She's fucking grieving. I can't say shit like that. "I shouldn't have said that. I'm sorry."

"Did you mean it?" She drops her eyes to the floor as her face flushes before flicking them back to me. "Did you mean what you just said, or is it some lame attempt at making me feel better?"

My mind races as I berate my wolf for coming to the surface and pushing me into breaking like that. Seeing the vulnerability in her eyes, I can't lie. Taking a deep breath to ground myself, I open my mouth and tell her the truth. "Every word."

I smile nervously, hoping she can see the truth in my eyes, the same truth I feel bone deep. "That day outside the shop, I saw the most beautiful woman on earth. You stole my heart and made me drop a carton of eggs." She giggles and the sound caresses my skin, causing goosebumps to rise on my arms. "I swear. I knew you were the one. Unfortunately, Theo stole your heart before I got the chance to." I shrug and take a long sip out of the mug in my hand in an effort to shut myself up.

She places her hand on top of mine. "I didn't know, Cain. Is… is that why you're always avoiding me?" She swallows and glances at her feet. "I thought you hated me."

Before I realise what I'm doing, my hand is running up her neck and her hair is falling through my fingers. "Never. I could never hate you."

My eyes lock onto her mouth, and I find myself inches away from her. Selena's tongue flicks out leaving a slight wetness behind, and I'm a goner. My lips crash onto hers, my tongue teasing at their seam. She parts her lips and I take that as an invitation. The sweet taste of hot chocolate and her honeysuckle scent explodes on my tongue.

I blindly place my mug on the table, wanting to run both my hands in her hair. My hands move to frame her face, her soft skin beneath my fingertips perfect.

She shifts, not breaking the kiss, and I hear a clunk as her mug connects with the table a second before her hands roam up my chest and lock around my neck. My wolf has practically melted, content to finally have our mate in our hands. Only she isn't our mate.

She's Theo's.

I break the kiss, jumping off the sofa and across the room, aiming to get some distance between us. "Shit! I'm sorry. You're my brother's girlfriend." I tug at my hair with my hands. "I shouldn't have done that." I pace in front of the French windows as I look out to the forest surrounding the house. I need to run. I should get as far away from her as possible.

Her hand on my back causes me to jump. I'd been so lost in my own head I hadn't even heard her move. "Cain. Please don't run."

Her choice of words has me turning. "Run?" I ask. Surely, she couldn't have meant—

She takes my hand in hers. "You look like you want to bolt. Please sit down again." Her pleading eyes have me moving towards the sofa and sitting down. "You're right. I'm with Theo and it's not fair to do this behind his back. I love him." Her words break my heart, but hearing the truth in them shatters it into a million pieces. A million pieces that will never be made into a whole again.

I nod, struggling to get words past the lump in my throat. "Let's put the TV on. Maybe we can find a good action movie or something."

Selena reaches for the remote and clicks through the TV channels, stopping on the first one that shows a screen full of explosions. A car crashes on screen and she flinches beside me before clearing her throat. "I think I'm going to go to bed. Will Theo mind if I sleep in his room?" She shuffles forward on the couch, readying herself to stand.

"Of course not." I grab the remote and turn off the TV. "I could do with an early night too. I'll show you up to his room." I run a hand through my hair as I stand, mentally berating myself at my idiotic offer—she's been dating him for over a year; she knows where his room is.

I hear the sofa crinkle as she stands. "Thanks."

I pause in front of Theo's room and open his door for her. "I'm just over there," I say, pointing to my door on the opposite wall up the hall. "If you need anything just give me a knock, okay?"

She smiles brightly and reaches out, taking the hand hanging at my side in hers. "Thank you for being there for me today, Cain. I appreciate it more than you'll know." She reaches up on her tiptoes to kiss me on the cheek. "When you meet 'the one' you're going to make her one happy girl." She drops my hand and walks into Theo's room, closing the door on me as I stare after her. I really hope she is a happy girl, or this last year of hell will have been for nothing.

The snick of my door opening rouses me from sleep. Sitting up, I tense, waiting to see if it's friend or foe. Selena's scent hits me and the tension in my body instantly floats away.

"Cain, are you awake?" she whispers, her voice barely audible.

"Yes. I'm awake." The shock of her arrival suddenly fades

and is replaced with worry as I wonder why she's coming to my room. "Are you okay?"

"Yes… no. Not really. Will you hold me? I feel so alone in there." Her voice breaks and I worry at my lip while considering her request. I'd love to hold her, but can I do it without taking it further? Without further murkying the water between us.

Taking a deep breath, I pat the bed beside me in invitation, forgetting that she can't see in the dark as well as I can. "Sure. Come and get in," I offer.

The door closes and I listen to her footsteps in the plush carpet as she makes her way towards me.

The bed dips and I hold the covers back as she slides in beside me. The T-shirt she's wearing goes down to her knees, and I know it must be Theo's. His scent wrapped around her helps me hold my wolf back. Yet another reminder that she isn't ours. *She's Theo's.*

Taking her into my arms, I pull her against me and settle down into the soft bed. Her breath becomes slow and steady, telling me she's drifted off to sleep.

I lie here, enjoying the feel of her body in my arms as the hours pass. I can't completely relax because I know if I do, my wolf may very well try to make the most of my unconscious state, and I can't allow that.

There's a loud crash on the stairs, and I gently release Selena, leaving her curled up in my bed as I head out of my room to see what's causing the noise. A glance at my watch tells me it's way too early to be Theo. It's only two in the morning.

I open the door and come face-to-face with my father. I see his nostrils flare as he takes in my half-dressed state. I'd gone to bed in just a pair of boxers and being a werewolf, you get used to being naked or half-naked around people. I'd not even considered pulling anything on when Selena had come in or just now when I'd gotten up.

"You fucker!" His fist flies at me, but I stop it in mine before it connects, his inebriated state having slowed his movements down. Some mean feat considering werewolves can't get drunk with alcohol. He's clearly had something. He's been known to get his hands on all kinds of drugs, ones that vets use on elephants. Even mixing the drugs together. He's always been a fucking dickhead, but since he lost his mate six months ago, he's been uncontrollable.

"It's not what you think, Dad." I shove him away from me as I pull the door behind me closed, not wanting him to disturb Selena. "You've got the wrong end of the fucking stick."

"She's been playing with your stick all right." His crude remark has him smirking. "It's okay, I won't tell Theo… as long as she gives my stick some attention too." He grabs at his crotch, emphasising his meaning

My fist flies at his vulgar display. The crunch as it connects with his jaw tells me something's broken. Pain surges through my hand, and I wonder if the crunch came from me or my father.

I glance at him on the floor as he shoves at his jaw, pushing it back into place with a grunt, unable to hide the pain. He gets to his feet slowly and steadily. The high he'd been riding will have been pushed away with the adrenaline now surging through him. My father glares at me in silence, his face turning red with anger as his energy pulses painfully against my skin.

My clenched fists shake at my sides. As much as I know I should never have attacked my father—my alpha—I can't help but feel I was in the right to do it. He's been a mess since Margie died, nothing but a burden on the pack. He shouldn't have said what he had about Selena, though. His own son's mate, or as good as. As these thoughts run through my mind, my back straightens and I lift my head, my eyes meeting his in a challenge.

"You better think long and hard for a second, Cain." His eyes bore into mine. "Back down now, because if you don't, I'll be forced to kill you and being my son won't save you from that. And that piece of skirt in there." He points to the door behind me. "She'll be fucking under me regardless of whether your brother takes her as a mate. I'm the alpha here." His lip turns up in a snarl. "Not him, and certainly not you."

I can see in his eyes he expects me to back down, but I can't. "You better go call in the pack. They all need to be here for an Alpha Duel." I stare him down until my eyes are stinging with the need to blink.

"So be it," he says, smirking as he pulls out his phone and walks away.

I head back into the bedroom and pace the room as my mind wanders. I have no fear for what tomorrow will bring. Tomorrow may be the end of my life, but I won't go out easily. I won't go out at all if I can help it.

It's been a long time since I last trained with Dad, just before he gave up training. *When you have a pack of werewolves to fight for you, what's the point in fighting for yourself?* He may even go into our duel tomorrow expecting one of his stronger wolves to stand in for him. Unfortunately, he's been a crap alpha lately, and I'm pretty sure he'll be sadly mistaken.

The only chance Dad has of beating me is if he draws on the power of the pack. Although he only has the ability to do that if the pack allows him to. I don't know if they would right now, so I could very well beat the old man tomorrow.

My wolf sits back, not caring about the fight ahead. It's going to happen and we can only deal with it at the time. There's no point worrying about it now. Liking this logic, I walk over to the bed and lay down beside Selena once again. I breathe in her scent knowing this will most likely be the last time I'll have her this close to me again.

———

The door clicks open and I jump up, alert, and ready to protect Selena from any advances my father may make. Unless he's here to kill me in my sleep having come to the conclusion he may actually have a tough fight on his hands when the duel comes.

The intruder's scent hits me and the tension leaves my body instantly. *Theo.*

"Hey. How's she doing?" He acknowledges Selena with a nod in her direction.

"She's…" I glance in her direction, memorising the sight of her on my bed. "She'll be glad you're back." I grab a pair of sweats off the chair by the wall and pull them on. "Go hug your girl. I'm done sleeping."

I consider telling him about Dad and the duel, but I can see his worry for Selena etched in the crease of his frown as he stares at her. I don't want to add to his stress or take away his attention from her. She needs him. Besides, there's nothing he can do to stop the duel.

5.

ALPHA DUEL

Theo catches me in the kitchen after lunch, finally having exited my bedroom and leaving Selena to shower. He claps a hand on my shoulder. "What have you done?" I start at the pressure of his hand, before he releases me. "Hey, I know it's something serious. I can feel it. The pack's energy through the bonds is beyond crazy, and yours isn't much better." He rubs at his forearms, no doubt rubbing my excess energy away as it brushes against his skin.

I hand him a coffee and pour another for myself. "I challenged Dad. He's calling in the pack and we'll be having an Alpha Duel tonight." I risk a look, flicking my eyes to his and see nothing but anger in his eyes.

"It should be me," he snaps, as he drives his fist into the countertop.

"You don't even know why I did it," I argue.

He takes a moment to sip his coffee, and I watch his eyes flicking from wolf to human as he pushes his wolf down. "It doesn't matter why. I should have done it a long time ago. He's been nothing but be a burden since Margie died."

Hearing his admission causes something deep inside me to settle. I know I'm doing the right thing, but hearing it from my big brother cements it inside me that little bit more.

"I can stand in for you. Challenge him myself," Theo offers.

"*No!* Don't you dare." I take a mouthful of coffee while I think carefully about my next words. "You take Selena away from here for a couple of hours. If I don't walk away from this, I don't want her to have to deal with the extra death on top of her family. Tell her... I've gone away." The thought of not making it causes my voice to break.

Theo pulls me into his arms, and I feel stupid hugging my brother. We're both fucking adults and we're hugging like babies. "I'm your big brother. I shouldn't let you do this."

I pull back and lock onto his eyes. "I need to do this for myself. I can't have you stand in for me. Promise me, Theo, look after that beautiful girl of yours."

He lets out a sigh, and after a moment's hesitation, he nods. "Fine. But you better beat the miserable old bastard." We break away, going back to our coffees.

I settle my arse against the countertop behind me. "I'll give it my all," I say, knowing I can't promise anything more.

"That's all I can ask." He weighs me up for minute, obviously thinking something over before nodding. "You'll make a good alpha if you do win."

I flinch, taken aback by his words. I wouldn't be alpha. I'd never take the pack. "No, Theo." I shake my head. "*You* would be a far better alpha than me, so I'd be handing the pack over to you." Winning an Alpha Duel would mean I'm entitled to the role of alpha, but Theo's older than me and far more deserving of the position. Not to mention he would be able to handle the stress of running a pack much easier than I would.

Theo's eyes widen, evidently surprised at my admission. "You mean that. I...." He releases a breath and gives me a heartwarming smile. "Thank you. It means a lot knowing you have so much faith in me."

Selena's scent fills the air a few seconds before she walks into sight behind Theo, effectively ending our conversation.

She wraps her arms around his waist, slipping by his side as Theo lifts his arm for her.

"Morning." She gives me a shy smile. "Thanks for last night."

"It was noth—"

She looks at me with a raised brow. "It *wasn't* nothing. Not to me," she snaps, cutting me off.

"Okay. Well… you're welcome then." I give Theo a pleading look and he quickly places a kiss on her temple.

"Dad's having a little get together later with some unsavoury characters." Theo throws me a wink she can't see. "I don't want them around you. So I was thinking, is there somewhere you'd like to go?"

"Actually, I'd like to go home. I don't know if I can stay there, but I will definitely need to pick some things up." She looks up at him with a solemn stare.

"Of course. Home it is." It's not like he'd deny her anything, let alone when she's looking at him like that. "I've just got to track Dad down to let him know our plans. He won't be happy we're leaving, but I honestly don't care what he thinks." He gives me one last look before walking out the room. Not knowing what the look was about, I grab a mug down and offer Selena a coffee.

"Yes, please. About last night… I…."

I shake my head. I really don't want to think about last night. I don't need thoughts of our kiss running through my mind. Not when I'm about to fight for my life. "Don't worry about last ni—"

She raises her voice over mine. "I heard you fighting with your dad. I didn't hear everything or even understand half of what I did hear, but I did hear what he said about me. Thank you for having my back. I know it must have caused trouble for you."

My face breaks into a smile. This beautiful woman always surprises me. "I'll always have your back. You're as good as my sister-in-law now." I throw her a wink and then almost bolt out of the room as I fight my wolf against releasing a growl. He did not like that statement one bit. I channel my anger, pushing it into my centre and hoping to hold onto it for later.

I glance at my watch for the fiftieth time—Nine fifteen. The pack started to arrive at seven in the evening, and they're still trickling in now.

My wolf has been pacing since my parting words to Selena at lunchtime. He isn't a patient soul, especially having to sit back and watch Theo with Selena most days.

Having her so close to me last night may have been a big mistake.

Unfortunately, I don't have the time to worry about that. I need to focus on the fight before me. *An Alpha Duel.*

Once my watch reads quarter to ten, I make my way to the clearing in the middle of the bush that surrounds the house. The fight is set for ten o'clock. Being tardy wouldn't really be an issue; it's not like there's any punishment he can give me. After all, he's going to try and kill me anyway.

As I walk through the last line of trees, all eyes fall upon me. It's hard to gauge in the bonds how everyone is feeling about our duel, but going by the occasional flat smile and nodding of heads I get as I pass, some of my pack mates must be happy with it. Let's just hope they'll get the outcome they want. I head to the centre and take off my shirt, throwing it to the ground as I wait for my opponent.

Chloe strides out of the crowd and stops before me. "Good luck, Cain." She lowers her voice to a whisper, obviously in the hope I'm the only one who can hear her next words. "The pack has needed a shake-up like this for a while."

I nod in agreement, and thank her for the luck she'd

offered. After giving me a quick peck on the cheek, she walks back to the crowd as Billy and Wes take her place beside me.

Wes claps a hand on my shoulder. "I don't know what provoked you to do this, but it's the right thing for the pack. You'll be a young alpha, but you have it in you to be a great one."

I let out a laugh. "I have to beat him first, Wes."

Billy looks at me with a raised brow. "You're a lot fitter than he is. You train every spare minute you get. I haven't seen your father train in years."

Pack members around us stir and we turn to see Dad strut through the parted crowd. A couple of the older wolves pat him on the back as he passes, offering him good wishes. It surprises me not more members follow with the action. I guess that in itself tells me just how much of the pack are wanting me to win today. He stops before us.

Billy and Wes both make a move to join the spectators, but Dad calls out. "Wes, we need a referee. I would've liked Theo to have the job but unfortunately, he's otherwise engaged." He looks at Wes with a raised brow. "Are you up for it?"

Wes's back stiffens at the request. "Of course. Are we ready?" he asks, looking between the two of us.

I grunt in answer.

"Let's get this over with," Dad says. There's no empathy in his voice. If he wins, he'll be killing his youngest son, and he doesn't seem to give a toss. *Bastard.*

Wes takes a moment to clear his throat before acknowledging the crowd. "Thank you for your patience tonight. We've been called here to play witness to an Alpha Duel. Cain Wilson has challenged the current alpha, his father, Marcus Wilson." He turns his attention to me. "Does the challenge still stand?"

"Yes." My words come out confident and clear. No one would know I'm worried about not making it through this fight. I've had duels before, but there's something in the air tonight. Some underlying current that makes me feel that this isn't anything like those regular duels.

The crowd stirs at my words and Wes turns his attention back to them. "Does anyone contest this duel?" Usually this line gives someone else the opportunity to fight me first. Either in hopes to weaken me for the fight with my real opponent or if not, kill me before I even get to fight my intended opponent. Most duels are to the death, but one can submit anytime during the fight if they wish to. That isn't the case in an Alpha Duel. This is to the death.

Everyone stands stock still. Even those that had wished Dad luck on his way in.

Dad stands taller than he had been before Wes's question, not showing any disappointment. Maybe he's happy to be fighting for himself.

"Marcus, will you be fighting as human or wolf?" Wes asks his voice bellows.

I tense as I wait for my dad's answer. It's well known that fighting in human form is more technical, and the winner would usually be more worthy of the win. Fighting in wolf form is dangerous, a stray claw caught in the wrong place could mean a quick death. It could go either way, and that seems too risky for my liking. I'd much rather a longer fight knowing I have the stamina to outlast my dad as well as the fighting skills to outmanoeuvre him.

"Wolf." That one word causes the crowd to go wild, because that means it will most likely be a bloody fight, and we are bloodthirsty creatures after all.

Wes gives me a worried glance. I guess we'd both been hoping Dad's answer would've been different.

I channel my wolf, allowing him to come to the forefront as I strip out of my remaining clothes. I can see my father already in his wolf form as I crouch down to all fours and feel my wolf take over my body completely.

Dad will have pulled on the powers of the pack to make his change instant, not even bothering to remove his clothes first.

I clench my teeth through the pain, not wanting to whimper and allow my father to consider it a weakness. After shaking off the last tingles of the change paw by paw, I look across to Wes.

"Ready?" he asks, turning from me to my father, trying to gauge how we may be feeling. He wouldn't be able to feel through the pack as clearly as an alpha would—it's usually the alpha who referees a duel for that reason.

We both snarl and turn to face each other.

"May the best man win," Wes announces as he steps back to the line of the crowd.

Dad pounces as soon as the words leave Wes's mouth, not giving me a chance to think about my movements.

I jump back out of reach and circle behind him. I'm not allowing him to win with a lucky shot. Everyone knows it's why he chose to fight in wolf form. I'll make him work for it.

He spins to face me, obviously not wanting me at his back, and snarls. His anger causes my fur to rise, but I don't let it distract me.

Pouncing on him and aiming for his neck, I end up with a mouthful of ear as he drops his head. His yelp of pain spurs me on to tear at it until it comes free, and I drop the piece of flesh to the ground.

He recovers quickly and throws out an identical manoeuvre.

Seeing it coming, I drop to my stomach, protecting my neck from his teeth, and then twist as he lands on top of me. My change in position throws him off target, and he scrambles for purchase as I flip onto my back and slide out from under him, ripping at his stomach with my claws as I go. Straightening up onto all fours, I jump back to get away from him in case he tries to attack.

I focus on my enemy to find him wavering on unsteady legs, blood dripping from underneath him, my claws having caused more damage than I'd thought. He howls, striking out for me sluggishly, seemingly using his last remnants of strength. I pounce sideways, hoping to get away before he hits. My side is suddenly searing in pain as his sharp teeth sink into my flesh. I bite back a whimper not wanting to give my opponent the confidence to keep fighting. His teeth connect with my ribs, and I brace myself, knowing he'll snap them to clear the way to my organs.

An excruciating burning sensation rolls over me, and I can't hold in the yelp this time. His jaws release me and I stumble back in a fog of pain, wanting to get as far away as possible, to give my head time to clear enough for me to focus on my next move.

I circle around him as he spins with me, not taking his eyes off me. I feign a lunge for his side. My teeth make contact, sinking into his throat. Coppery blood fills my mouth; his artery is pumping out his blood faster than he can heal. He slackens beneath me and I drop him to the ground, finally relaxing in the knowledge that I've won.

Wes appears before me, hands stretched out, showing he means me no harm. It throws me for a second. *I know he wouldn't hurt me, so why gesture?*

Hearing a fierce snarling, I glance around the crowd to look for the wolf it belongs to, only to find the pack members on their knees with their heads dropped in submission—every single one of them.

I suddenly realise it's me who's snarling. I immediately rein in my wolf, persuading him to retreat as I shift back to my human form, which comes easier than usual. It still hurts, but it takes a fraction of the time, quite unusual when you counter in the fact that I'm injured, which would usually slow the process down even more. I shake the thought off along with the tingles running over my skin from the change and turn to Wes, who's now bent over my dad.

"Is he…?" I start to ask as I reach through the bonds to feel for my father. He's no longer there. Just an empty space where he used to be.

Wes turns at my words, staying low to the ground in submission. "I pledge my loyalty to you, Cain Wilson. The new Alpha of the Mount Roxby Pack."

With his words, something stirs through the pack bonds. They alter as each pack member around me mutters the same words, and I suddenly become the centre of the pack, filling the space my father had vacated.

"I, Cain Wilson, live to protect the Mount Roxby Pack and its members." The words leave my mouth before I can even register them. In the silence that follows, I wonder if I've done the right thing. Theo should be alpha. He's older, wiser, not to mention stronger.

Theo's not here, my wolf reminds me, and I understand why he jumped in and claimed the pack, taking the choice out of my hands.

The pack needs an alpha in this moment, and I'm the rightful one to fill the hole.

6.

SIN BEFORE MARRIAGE

CAIN - SIX YEARS AGO

A year after fighting my father and handing the pack over to Theo, it's the eve of his wedding, and I find myself in the worst place I could possibly be—standing before his blushing bride-to-be in an empty house.

"Where is everyone?" I glance behind Selena at the large open-space living area, hoping to see someone, yet knowing I won't because I can only feel her energy. Meaning we're the only two people in the house. "I thought some of the girls were staying over?"

She laughs whilst walking over to the sofa. "I told Alyssa to go to Wes. You know what those two are like, forever on each other's minds." She pulls a blanket over her lap as she settles herself into her spot. "Chloe had a date." Selena glances at me and winces. "I'm sorry. I know you two have been on and off lately. I...."

I shake my head. "Hey, it's fine. We were never anything serious." Telling her the only woman I've ever wanted to be serious about is her, is on the tip of my tongue, but I swallow it down.

The tension leaves her shoulders and she pats the spot next to her in invitation. "So, we've discovered why I'm a loner. What about you? Why aren't you at the hotel boozing it up with Theo?" She turns her body to face me, giving me her undivided attention.

Unsure what to say, I bide my time, glancing around the room at the TV. Seeing Ian Somerhalder on the screen, I know she's watching her favourite show, *The Vampire Diaries*, and missing it since it's on mute. "Hey, you're missing sexy Damon. I'm certainly not as interesting as him."

Her laugh sends chills over my body. "Damon may be mighty sexy, but I care about you and why you're not having fun like you should be," she says, as she playfully nudges me with her blanket-covered foot.

To be honest, I don't really know why I came. I just needed to be here. I open my mouth to tell her as much when something completely different comes out. "I need to show you something."

I look to the door sharply, expecting to see someone there speaking instead of myself. The words register in my mind and I instantly know why I came tonight. She has no idea about the existence of werewolves, yet by this time tomorrow, she'll be tied to one for the rest of her life. Married to Theo, an alpha werewolf. The danger that brings her way... she deserves to know it beforehand.

"This sounds serious." The concern in her voice has me kicking myself before I've even started. What if I scare her and she runs away from Theo? She doesn't have anyone but us.

I debate internally on how to tell her. Where to start. Deciding against an immediate show and tell, I take a deep breath and jump in at the deep end.

"Have you ever noticed anything strange about us? Theo, me, some of our friends?"

She frowns, her cute little nose crinkling slightly as she thinks about my question. "Not that I can think of. There are a lot of you and you're all really close. But... nothing strange. No."

"I don't know how to tell you this." I rub the back of my neck with a hand. "Jesus, who'd have thought this would be so hard?" I joke before trying a new tact, having gotten an idea from her favourite show flicking across the TV screen. "Have you ever wondered where those stories come from?" I point to the screen which now has a werewolf character on it, front and centre. "Werewolves and vampires," I clarify.

Her brow creases once again, and I can see the deep thought on her face. "Well, I guess some people have good imaginations?" She ends the sentence high as though it's a question.

"What if I tell you they aren't just some creative peoples' made-up story? What if I tell you they're real?" I stare at her intently, wishing for her to believe me.

Her eyes widen in surprise. "If you weren't the most serious person I've ever met, I'd be worried you're playing some kind of trick on me. But you don't do pranks." She's right in the fact that I don't do pranks, not since meeting and losing her anyway. She takes a deep breath and levels me with a soul-searching stare. "Let's say I believe you. I guess they could exist. Why is that so important on the night before my wedding?"

After taking a quick, grounding breath, I blurt it out. "You're marrying one, Selena. Theo's a werewolf. We all are."

She scoots back on the sofa, giving me as much distance as she possibly can. Her fear is palpable against my skin.

"Please don't be scared. You've known us for a long time and we haven't harmed you," I beg, my heart hurting at the thought of scaring her.

"I'm not scared of you, Cain. I'm scared that the only people I care about in the world have lied to me for the last two years." The sadness in her voice cuts me in two, and I suddenly think I'd rather her be scared of me.

I reach out, taking her hand in mine, not bothering to slow my supernatural movement now the cat's out of the bag. "Selena… please don't hate me. Or at least don't hate Theo for it." I snatch my hand back, angry at myself. It shouldn't matter if she hates me, but it does. She picks up my hand and gives it a reassuring squeeze. "Our existence is a big secret. We're ordered by our alphas to never tell anyone."

"Alphas?" she asks tentatively.

"An alpha is the leader, the boss of the wolf pack, or family. He keeps the pack members in line, making sure nobody endangers the pack or humans." I greedily take in her features with my eyes, trying to gauge how well she's following.

"Are you all related? The pack." The word rolls off her tongue without confidence, like she's unsure of the word.

I shake my head, no. "We're made up of lots of different families. Like a tight-knit community."

She nods her acceptance, and before I can carry on, she asks another question. "So, if Theo couldn't tell me because of his alpha's order, how come you can?"

I'd wondered how long it would take her to get to the tricky questions. I stand up and start to pace the room, taking the moment of silence to think my words over before I speak them. "There's a loophole, so to speak. Do you believe in soul mates?" I stop my pacing and pin her with a stare, needing to see the truth in her answer.

She swallows and nods. "Yes, I did, but now I'm wondering if I was being a fool."

"Every wolf has a mate who belongs to them. Their true mate. Some wolves are lucky enough to grow up with their mate knowing them for their whole lives. Others find them somewhere down the track." I take a calming breath before speaking my next words. "Unfortunately, that means there are the unlucky ones who never find them, too. There comes a time in a wolf's life when he needs to decide whether he should persevere to find his true mate or to choose a suitable mate for himself." I catch sight of Selena watching me intently as I pace. "Theo decided to choose you over searching."

Her gasp of hurt causes me to want to slap myself. I should have handled that better. Of course, she thought she was his mate. "I'm not...."

"No, I'm sorry." I run my hands through my hair and tug at it, trying to free my frustration.

Her hand rests on top of mine, and she eases the grip I have on my hair. "Don't harm yourself, Cain. I know you didn't mean to upset me."

The fact that my words caused her pain, hurts me so much more than any tugging on my hair could have done. If only I could show her that. *We can.* My wolf's words run through my head, and I contemplate them for a second. *What good would telling her do?*

If I say the words out loud, claim her out loud, it will only cause pain for me and most probably her too.

She'll know she's someone's mate. She'll know she is so much more than unimportant.

I frame her face in my hands and beg, "Tell me you feel it."

"Feel it?" Her furrowed brow tells me it's all one-sided.

Needing to spell it out, I go on. "The attraction between us. Tell me you fucking feel it too." My wolf paces inside me, waiting for her answer, lacking his usual confidence in the matter.

She smiles, but it doesn't reach her eyes, causing my heart to plummet. She's going to let me down. "Of course, I feel it." Her sadness is palpable. "Ever since that first day we met. But... I'm with Theo, and I...."

I search her eyes and finish the sentence for her. "Love him." We sigh in unison. "I love him too. That's why I've never claimed you, even though I know you're my true mate."

Her eyes widen in surprise. "Your true mate?" She whispers so quietly I can only just hear it, even with my supernatural hearing. "Me?" she asks a little louder.

"Yes." A weight seems to lift off my shoulders as I say the

word. I can breathe again, having finally spilt the beans. I've been so weighed down hiding my secret and I hadn't even realised, until now. I point to the couch. "Shall we sit again? I guess I have a lot to explain."

She nods, and we both take our seats. Selena shuffles back into the corner once again to face me better.

Taking a calming breath, I go on. "That first day I saw you, I knew you were meant for me. Your scent does things to me." I inhale, breathing her scent in, allowing my eyes to close as a smile crosses my face, not at all conscious of showing her the reaction I'm talking about. "I left that day with a plan to come back in the morning and woo you."

Selena frowns. "But you didn't."

I sigh. "No, I didn't. When I got home, Dad sent me to do business with another pack. I arrived back to find Theo had a new girlfriend. *You.*" I let out a sad laugh as I look at my fisted hands. "My mate was no longer mine to claim." I can't help but be mad at my father for sending me away at such a pivotal moment in my life. If only he'd listened to me that night, my life could be so different now.

Selena's hand brushes mine. My eyes come back to watch her flatten my fists as she takes my hands in hers, pulling them into her lap and shuffling closer towards me. "Cain, I don't understand the whole werewolf and true mate thing but, if the pain and sadness I can see in your face and body are anything to go by, I know it's taken a lot for you to live like this. Why didn't you tell me or Theo earlier?"

I turn her hand over in mine and trace her lifeline with my index finger. "Because Theo was happy. For the first time that I could remember, he was fucking happy. He made you happy too. I couldn't take that away from you both." I slide my hand up her arm and edge closer to her on the sofa. "I wish I could be selfish and take you. Claim you. But I can't. It's too late for that now." I feel my wolf at the surface. He wants to claim her regardless of the consequences.

Selena's widening eyes tell me she can see him in my eyes before the change in my eyesight registers with me. "You're not Cain," she states, surprising me by not cowering from us as I'd imagined she would if she ever saw my wolf.

"No." Selena flinches at the change in my voice as my wolf talks to her. "I won't hurt you," he says. Both of us wait on tender hooks to see how she'll react.

Her shy smile and relaxing posture go a long way to calm both my wolf and me down. I find myself leaning closer to her as her tongue pokes out and licks her bottom lip. Still in control, my wolf takes advantage of this moment, taking her mouth with mine in a fierce kiss. She melts into me willingly as my wolf slips back into his hiding place, handing me control of myself once again. Addicted to the taste of her honeysuckle scent, I take as much as she is willing to give me. It's been such a long time since I've tasted her lips, it invigorates me. I feel like I haven't been living all this time I haven't been tasting her. Selena's hand roaming up my chest spurs me on, and I sink my hands in to her hair as I pull her closer towards me. There's no turning back now. Not for me. I need to have my fill while I can.

Selena pulls back, breaking our kiss and I let her go—this isn't a good idea anyway. It will only lead to pain and heartbreak for us all. She reaches her hand down to her waist and pulls the tie on her silk robe, revealing her hourglass figure and erasing any thoughts I had of ending this.

I brush my hands over her shoulder as I push her robe off, leaving it to drop to the sofa. "You're absolutely stunning." She looks even more magnificent than I'd imagined in all of my fantasies.

A blush runs across her face, but she doesn't try to cover up. She kneels on the sofa before me, allowing me to take her in with my eyes. I trail my hand down over her chest and caress a circle around her nipple.

"Your touch feels so good." She tilts her head back and closes her eyes, seemingly basking in the feel of my touch. "It's almost like electricity running over my skin." She's feeling the mate connection between us as I touch her.

Part of me knows I should stop my ministrations and explain it to her, but I also know if I do, I would never start again. Leaning forward, I take the pink bud into my mouth as I allow my finger to trace circles around the other one. The needy moan that leaves her throat tells me I did the right thing. I lower her back so she's lying on the sofa without breaking the seal between my mouth and her breast. She opens her legs to give me room between them, and my attention shifts to her other nipple.

Her hands roam over my shoulders. "Take it off, Cain." She tugs at my cotton tee. "Please. I need to feel your skin."

Needing to give her exactly what she wants, I grab the material at the back of my neck and I pull it over my head, throwing it across the room as she runs her hands over my chest and abs. My wolf growls his appreciation. Her wide eyes tell me I allowed the sound to escape my mouth, and I give her a sheepish smile before crushing my mouth against hers whilst her hands make quick work of my button-up jeans.

7

TOO MUCH INFORMATION

"Fucking hell, Cain. I don't need to hear the gory details." Theo's voice pulls me back to the present. "I may be married to someone else now, but I don't need to hear the ins and outs of you cheating with my ex-wife the night before our wedding." He shakes his head as though to jiggle away the thoughts.

Sometime during my story, I'd perched on the edge of Theo's desk. I glance down at the ball of rubber bands I've been nervously rolling between my fingers. "Sorry, I didn't think about TMI. I just wanted to tell you everything at last."

Theo releases a short sigh. "Well, one mystery is solved at last." I frown at him, unsure what mystery he's talking about. "I know why we suddenly had a new sofa after the wedding. What the hell did you do with the old one?"

I laugh at the memory of that night and the realisation of the task before me—in keeping our betrayal a secret. After the night's events, if a wolf had walked into the house, they would've smelt what we'd been up to. Selena's scent and mine would be mixed together along with the tell-tale scent of sex. It was all over the sofa. "After..." I pause. Knowing he doesn't want to hear the details, I hold back on spelling the situation out. "Selena told me that it changed nothing. She loved you with everything she had and wanted to marry you the next day." My heart aches at the memory, even with the time that has passed. "She didn't want anyone to find out, so I had to do everything I could to make sure it stayed between us. That meant the sofa had to go."

"Is that why you didn't turn up for your best man duties?" Theo asks. His sadness fills the room, becoming so thick in the air it feels like I'm choking. I cough, trying to once again breathe.

The guilt that runs through me reminds me of my reasons for missing my brother's wedding. "I couldn't face you, and to be honest, I didn't know if my wolf would sit back and allow the wedding to go ahead if I were there. I needed to stay away for everyone's sake." I rub a hand over my face, trying to wipe away the tiredness that I've been collecting over the years. I've never fully been able to drop the guilt I've been carrying.

Theo's arms wrap around me in a hug. "It's okay, little brother. You don't need to feel guilty anymore," he says, having clearly sensed it through the pack bonds. I give him a quick pat on the back and he pulls away. "I can't believe Selena has known about us all this time and just played along pretending she didn't." He shakes his head in disbelief. "Why didn't she tell me? There were so many times she could have used it as ammo against me. Especially towards the end when we constantly argued."

"Most probably because I told her how dangerous it was for her to know." Thinking back on it, maybe I shouldn't have told her. If she'd used that ammo in the heat of an argument like Theo had suggested, she could have been killed.

Just the thought has my wolf on edge, has him wanting to break free and fight off anyone who may harm our mate. I close my eyes and take a deep breath.

Theo's hand rests on my shoulder, his energy giving me the power to push my wolf back.

"Thank you," I say, opening my eyes and locking them with his.

He drops his hand from my shoulder. "You've been a lone wolf for far too long. I think you need us as much as we need you." He pours us both another drink.

Taking the glass, I swirl the drink around as I contemplate his words. "So, you still want me to stay?"

"Of course, I do. Hell, I want you to stay more than I did before you started talking." He laughs. "Who would have thought, telling me about how you slept with my wife could have such a happy outcome?" I laugh along with him. It is kind of crazy when you put it that way. "The only issue now is how are you going to claim your mate?"

I shake my head in disbelief at how this is all turning out. "Selena's a runner. She isn't going to welcome me with open arms." I sigh. It's going to take time. But if I'm taking Theo up on his offer, I'll have plenty of time and we'll be under the same roof, so there'll be plenty of opportunities to win her trust.

I guess I owe thanks to Theo and Bel for not slamming the door in her face when she turned up on their doorstep, pregnant and homeless. From what I've heard, she'd returned hoping he would take her back and be willing to raise another man's child. Which knowing Theo and the fact he's always wanted to start a family, he would have done just that… if he hadn't already found Bel.

Theo spins his glass in his hand, his eyes pinned to the amber liquid swirling around it. "How do you feel about the bringing up another man's baby?"

Lifting my eyes, I lock them on his, hoping he can see my certainty. "A stranger may have brought the baby into existence, but it will be mine and my mate's baby in all the ways that matter.

Theo downs his drink and pats me on the back. "Drink up.

We've got a grieving pack to deal with, and you've got a woman's heart to win."

With a smile, I salute him with my glass before downing it. As I grab my bag from the floor, I revel in the settled feeling that flows through me. I have a pack. I instantly realise Theo was right: I've been a lone wolf for far too long.

8.

CAT'S DON'T LIKE BAGS

SELENA

I stop in my tracks as I face my biggest mistake. To this day, my heart and head can't decide whether the mistake was sleeping with him or letting him go.

I've been avoiding him since he first arrived back in town. The day I came face-to-face with him after all this time… my God, I felt like running for the hills. Most of me still feels like running, but that little piece of me, the tiny bit that thinks letting him go was the mistake, keeps me here. Well that, and the life growing inside me. I need to stay here for him or her. I've got friends and support here in Mount Roxby. Even if they did come from a failed marriage. As soon as I'm able to work and get some money behind me, I'll find my own place. I'm just grateful that Theo and his new wife, Bel, are willing to let me stay under their roof for the time being. I'm not sure I'd be as understanding if I were in their shoes.

"Selena." My name rolling off his tongue makes my legs turn to jelly. I've missed him saying my name.

"Cain," I breathe his name. It's barely a whisper but I know he'll hear it with his wolf's hearing. He's the only one who knows I'm aware of their secret. After all, he told it to me years ago, but he also told me we'd both be in danger if anyone found out. So I never let on that I knew, not even after I was married to Theo.

Cain's eyes drop to the hand resting on my growing stomach. "How far along are you?"

I look down at the bump in question and stroke it lovingly. I've found myself doing it more and more as it's grown. "Seven months. I already look like a beached whale. I dread to think how I'll look nearer my due date."

"You couldn't look anything but beautiful." The words seem to leave his mouth before he realises what he's saying. He clears his throat and drops his eyes to his feet.

My eyes follow his. Spotting the bag at his feet, my heart sinks. *He's leaving again?*

"No. Not anymore." His answer has me snapping my eyes back to his. I register I must have said the question out loud. "I'm needed here. Wes…." He doesn't finish the sentence, but I was here when it happened. Wes has been killed and somehow, they all knew without even receiving a phone call. It was as if they were psychic. Obviously, it has to be a wolf thing, and it's not like I couldn't question it. In fact, I have a feeling they've forgotten I'm still here.

But Cain knows.

"So, he is… dead." I struggle to say the word. The last time I had to think about that word, I'd lost my baby brother and father.

The grim look on his face is answer enough, but he still gives me a quick nod.

"I'm sorry. He was…." Glancing around, I spot people looking at us, clearly eavesdropping, and I let my sentence fade off. I don't want to say anything that could alert them to me knowing their secret.

"Pack. Yes. He was beta, which is a huge part of the pack. Theo's…." The horror must show on my face because he reaches out and takes my arm as my legs wobble threatening to give way. I've kept this secret for so long. Now he's going to get us both killed. He pulls me towards the window seat. "Sit down before you fall down. Then tell me what made you look so terrified."

I glance around the large formal dining room again and notice one of the guys glaring at Cain. "You said…" I lower my voice. "Pack."

"Oh." He laughs. "That cats out the bag now, beautiful. I've just spent the last hour telling Theo everything."

My eyes well with tears. "Everything?" I repeat, as dread fills me. He's in a world of trouble and it's all my fault.

He crouches before me and brushes away a tear as his hands frame my face. "Don't look so worried. Everything is going to be fine. No one will be upset with you. Okay?" He clearly has the wrong end of the stick. I'm not worried about me.

I pin him with a stern look. "It's not me I'm worried about. What's going to happen to you?" I bite my lip in concern, part of me not wanting to hear his answer.

"I told you a long time ago, I was the only person who *could* tell you. You're my true mate, and whether I've claimed you or not, I'm allowed to tell you." He pops my lip from between my teeth with his forefinger. "So, stop chewing on that poor lip."

I lift my hands and wipe at my eyes, feeling marginally better. "He'll hate me. Oh God… the night before the wedding. And I've lied all this time, pretending not to know." I hide my face in my hands as thoughts of Theo kicking me out of his home and running me out of town run through my mind.

"I don't hate you, Selena. In fact, it helps me forgive you." Theo's voice has me peeking out from between my fingers. He's crouched before me where Cain had been only moments ago.

"Really?" I ask. Seeing him smiling at me genuinely helps me relax. I slowly drop my hands from my face.

"Yes. I understand why you and Cain did what you did. Neither of you had a choice in the matter. You were meant for each other. It's as simple as that."

Meant for each other. Is it really that easy? If we were meant for each other, wouldn't we be together now? The thought makes my heart ache.

Part of me wants to look around for Cain, to see if Theo's words hurt him as much as they do me, but I don't. Instead, I give Theo a smile that I'm not really feeling. "Thank you."

Looking in his emerald eyes makes me remember how much I loved him. He is the one person who made me believe the saying "one's eyes are the window to one's soul." His eyes say so much.

"I did love you… so much. I hope you don't question that." I feel the need to make him understand. I wipe a tear from my eye and look away. Seeing a number of people looking at us, my stomach sinks as I'm suddenly aware we aren't the only ones in the room. *How could I have forgotten?*

"I don't, Lena." The nickname he used to call me has me snapping my attention back to him. He really doesn't hate me. "You wouldn't have stuck around if you didn't love me."

I give him a genuine smile as a weight I didn't realise I was carrying lifts from my shoulders.

Feeling freer than I have for as long as I can remember, I glance around the room, and for the first time tonight, I really see the people here. See the solemn expressions on everyone's faces. And I realise it doesn't take a werewolf to feel the sadness in the room. The loss of Wes has hit everyone hard. "How's Alyssa?" I ask, knowing what the answer will be before the words leave my mouth.

Theo sighs as he stands and then sits beside me in the window seat. "She's a mess. She can't bear to be near any of us. It just makes her miss him more."

I nod, conscious of what it's like to grieve someone. "She needs to deal with her own grief before she can deal with all of yours."

"How did you know that?" The surprise I hear in the high pitch of his voice has me turning to look at him.

I shrug. "My dad went through the same thing when we lost Mum. It was a hard couple of years."

He nods. "Of course. I'm sorry."

I place my hand on his forearm. He always seemed to be comforted by touch. "It was a long time ago." A throat clears, and I glance up to see Bel step up beside Theo, causing me to remove my hand quickly. I don't want her to get the wrong idea. I give her a quick smile before speaking again. "If Alyssa can't handle being around the pack, she's not going to be able to go home. Where will she be staying?"

"As much as that statement has me wanting to ask a number of questions, the main one being the fact that Selena seems to know about the pack, I'm going to let that slide because I want to know the answer to Selena's question more." Bel prods Theo in the arm. "But you better fill me in later."

Theo pulls Bel into his lap, enticing a laugh from her. Watching them like this, I can't help but think they really are made for each other.

"I wouldn't dream of keeping you out of the loop," he says, giving her a quick peck on the cheek before turning his attention back to me. "I've sent her to a safe house. It's one we haven't used before, so there will be no wolf scents inside."

"Is she on her own?" Bel asks frantically. "She shouldn't be on her own."

Theo rubs a hand down Bel's bicep. "Hey. You know I wouldn't leave her alone. Jared's with her. He's going to stay for as long as she needs." Bel relaxes in Theo's arms and hearing his words, I relax too. Having lived in the same house as Jared for a while now, I know Alyssa will be well looked after. He's a protector, not unlike Theo.

"I'd like to go and visit her. Maybe give her another shoulder if she needs one." Theo looks at me with distant eyes, making me think he must be weighing up my plan. "We were close once, and I'm not part of the pack."

He nods. "You might be right. Give me your phone and I'll put the address in."

I glance around, feeling somewhat stupid. "I don't have a phone." Theo and Bel glance at each other, both frowning. "I don't have anyone to keep in contact with." I swallow and lower my voice, feeling vulnerable and somewhat ashamed. "I don't have any friends."

"Here." A phone is held out across me, towards Theo. "Put it in mine. I'll take her," Cain says as Theo takes the phone and starts tapping at the screen. Cain's fingers brush my shoulder and I look up.

"I'm perfectly fine getting myself there if you have things to do." I glance around the room at the people filling it. The room has a sorrowful feel to it, although people are chatting whilst giving small touches here and there—comforting each other.

"I'm sorry, Selena, but I don't think you'll get that bump behind the steering wheel." Theo's words have me snapping my attention his way. He might as well have said I was a beached whale. Although, he's right. The last time I drove it wasn't exactly comfortable being squeezed behind the wheel, not that I'll let him know that.

Bel smacks him in the chest. "I can't believe you just said that." She turns to me, a blush on her cheeks as she smiles, obviously embarrassed by her husband's comment. "Don't listen to him, Selena. He can be so insensitive sometimes."

Cain holds his hand out to me. "Shall we?" Taking his hand, I use everything I have not to groan as I stand. I may feel and look like a beached whale, but I don't need someone else to point it out. I do have some dignity.

We barely make it two steps before we're stopped by Frankie and Jesse. From what I've read between the lines, they're from Western Australia. I'm assuming another pack, since Jesse has the same intense feeling that Theo and Cain both give off. Frankie is different. She has a warmth to her the others don't. Not even the women in Theo's pack. Frankie had been missing, and somehow Cain ended up finding her. She's timid around everyone except Cain, even her husband, Jesse. I can't help but feel jealous of the connection she has with Cain. *Have they slept together?* It's irrational; it's not as if Cain's mine. Hell, I'm his brother's ex-wife. I have no right at all to be turning all hulk over thoughts like that.

"Cain," Frankie says quietly as she edges forward towards his already open arms. It's like he knew she wanted a hug without her even suggesting it. Like I said, they have a unique connection.

"Hey, darling." Cain greets her as she settles in his arms, her head tucked nicely under his chin.

I watch her husband and can't help but wonder if he's feeling jealous, too. The tightness of his jaw and clenching of his fists at his sides confirms my thoughts. Jesse closes his eyes and takes a deep breath. Upon opening them, he looks behind me, and I can only guess he's looking at Theo. With a sharp nod, he walks past me.

"We're leaving," Frankie says, lifting her chin to look up at Cain. "Theo needs to focus on the pack and I don't think he can, not with another alpha in his territory." She lets out a small sigh. "And to be honest, Jesse's struggling having me around all these wolves we don't know." She rests her head back on his chest and he gently rubs her back.

"I'm going to miss you and Angel. Give her a kiss from me." He smiles the sweetest smile as he talks about Angel. I can't help but wonder who she is? The green-eyed monster comes through even stronger than before.

"We'll miss you, too. You could always come back with us." I can hear the eagerness in her voice, but it seems to make Cain stiffen.

"You don't need me anymore, darling. You've got Jesse and his whole pack." He pulls her off his chest and holds her at arm's-length leaning down to get to her eye level.

I look around the room, wondering whether I should leave? I feel like I'm intruding on something intimate.

"You've got to let him in, Frankie. It's the only way you can both heal," Cain's says, his tone soft yet insistent.

She nods. "I know." I watch entranced as a tear runs down her cheek. Cain's quick to wipe it away before giving her a kiss on the forehead.

I feel a hand brush my back and I jump, my hands going straight to my stomach, protecting my baby. "Sorry. It's Selena, isn't it?" Jesse asks as he steps around me holding his hands up in an "I'm not going to harm you" gesture. I nod. "There's just a lot of people in here. It's hard not to touch people as you pass."

I smile and relax, lowering my hands to my sides. "That's okay. I was away with the fairies," I say, offering an excuse for me jumping. I can't exactly say I was spying on his wife and Cain.

"Hey, mate." Cain offers Jesse his hand, and they pull each other into one of those one-armed slap-on-the-back man hugs. "Have a safe trip back."

"Thanks… for everything, Cain." Jesse looks in the direction of Frankie. "I don't know…" He looks back at Cain, piercing him with his solid stare. "…what I would have done if you ha—"

"We've had this conversation already." Cain cuts him off as they release each other's hands.

Jesse holds his hand out towards Frankie. Watching through the gap between Cain and Jesse, I see her look at his hand for a second before taking it loosely in hers. He offers her a warm smile before turning his attention back to Cain. "You'll always be welcome in my territory. And if things don't work out here, there's a place for you in my pack."

Cain steps back. "Thank you, Jesse. I really appreciate your offer, but I've got things I need to do here," he says, the pitch of his voice tells me he must be surprised at the offer. "In saying that, when you find that bastard, I'll be more than happy to jump on the next plane to help you out."

Frankie tenses and Jesse strokes her arm with his spare hand. "Thanks. Theo gave us the same offer."

Cain laughs. "I'm pretty sure the whole pack would be ready to hightail it to Perth."

With one last handshake, Jesse turns to leave, his hand on the small of Frankie's back gently guiding her ahead of him. Frankie suddenly stops, and I think she's going to give Cain one last hug as she turns, but her arms are suddenly around my neck. "Look after him, Selena." With those four whispered words, she releases me and is out of sight before I can question what she meant by them.

9

PRECIOUS CARGO

CAIN

Standing at the gate, I watch as Selena knocks on the door. She turns to look at me, and I wonder if she can feel my eyes on her. "I'm okay, you know. You can wait in the car."

I sigh. She might be okay, but I can't bear to let her out of my sight.

The door opens and I hear Jared's deep voice. "Selena." He glances at me, then back at Selena. "What can I do for you?"

"I was hoping to see Alyssa. To let her know she isn't alone."

Jared lets out a rumble deep in his chest. "She isn't alone." The force of his anger prickling against my skin has me stepping up beside Selena.

Selena's hand reaches out to stop me stepping in front of her. "Don't, Cain. He isn't going to hurt me." Jared steps back, his jaw slack and eyes wide in what I can only assume to be shock.

"My b— Wait…." He looks at Selena, an eyebrow raised in question.

"Oh. Yes, I know. It's a long story. I've known about your secrets for a long time." She frowns. "Well, not yours, but his." She points a thumb in my direction.

Jared glances at me, and I give him a quick nod in agreement. "Well, in that case, I'll be straight with you both. My beast is close to the surface. It's the only way I'm managing to keep Alyssa from shifting. Her wolf keeps trying to make her shift in her sleep." My gaze drifts over him. The stiffness of his body and his golden lion eyes on his face tells me how truthful his words are.

I grab Selena's hand in mine. "I think we should go. We can come back another day when things are a little calmer." *Mainly Jared.*

Jared's head tilts as though he's listening to something inside the house. "It sounds like she's waking up. Come in. I'll go see if she's up for visitors." He glances at me sharply. "Are you part of the pack still?"

"Faintly," I admit, wondering if Alyssa would be able to feel me through whatever is left of the bonds. I can barely feel them myself.

He bites at the inside of his cheek whilst he thinks. "Come in. I'll let her know who's here."

We follow him in, stopping in the small lounge as he walks further into the house. There's a mustard-coloured sofa facing a large TV, which is hanging on the pristine white wall. The faint smell of paint leaves me wondering whether it's a recent refurbishment. I'll have to ask Theo about it. If he's still doing refurb's, I could probably help him out and make myself some money at the same time.

"Sit! Your feet will thank you for it," I suggest, catching Selena's longing look at the sofa.

She opens her mouth speak, but Jared comes back in the room causing her to quickly snap it shut again. "Cain, she doesn't feel comfortable seeing you, but she said you could go into the bedroom to see her, Selena." He points in the direction he'd just come back from. "It's the last door on the right."

She looks at him sheepishly through her lashes. "Is there a bathroom I can dash in on the way?" She points to her bulging belly. "This little monster is right on my bladder."

"Of course. First door on the left." Jared walks over to the sofa and takes a seat. Following his lead, I lower myself into the armchair to the side of the sofa, angled to face the side of the coffee table.

"She'll be safe? Alyssa won't shift without you there?" I hear the worry in my voice and cough to try and cover it. Surely Alyssa wouldn't hurt Selena—a human.

He closes his eyes and takes a deep breath. "She's in control for now. I'll sense it and will be able to send my energy to her before Selena is in any danger." He opens his eyes, showing me the golden orbs of his lion once again. "I wouldn't have let you in the house if I thought Selena or the baby would be in any danger." I nod, taking him at his word. "Alyssa looked panicked at the thought of being close to another wolf. She might not be able to sense you through the pack bonds, but she'd be able to feel your wolf against her skin and she wouldn't be able to handle that right now."

I raise a brow at him. "But she's okay with your lion?"

His energy flares and brushes against my skin making my wolf stand to attention. He grins. "He feels nothing like a wolf."

"I guess you're right." I glance up the hallway once again, wondering how things are going in there. "Theo will appreciate all you're doing for her. The whole pack will."

Jared sighs. "I'm not doing it for Theo or his pack. I'm doing it for Alyssa." He frowns. "She needs someone, and if I can fill that position, I'll do it for as long as I'm needed to."

I finally relax in his company, realising he's a bona fide good guy. "I can see why Theo lets you stay around even though you're Bel's ex." I give him a genuine smile. "You're a good guy."

"That he is," Selena says as she shuffles back into the room. "Alyssa asked for you. She can't sleep in the empty bed. She thought..." She glances at me and then back to Jared before finishing her sentence. "She thought she might be able to sleep next to your beast."

Jared nods. "I was planning on offering to do that anyway."

We both stand. "We'll let ourselves out," Selena offers, glancing at the door. "We can lock the door behind us."

Jared leans in and gives her a gentle hug. "Thank you, Selena. You take care of yourself." His eyes drop to her belly. "And the little one."

Selena laughs. "Little… it's far from little. But I will. I'm sure Cain and the pack will be keeping an eye on me." She glances shyly at me, and I give her a wink. Of course I'll be watching over her. I'm aiming to win her heart this time. Jared nods and heads towards the hallway and Alyssa.

We walk out the door and Selena pauses just as I'm about to close it. "Do you have Jared's number?"

I frown, wondering why she'd want his number. Jealousy raises its ugly head for a second, but I quickly snuff it out as I tell myself to stop being stupid. "No, but Theo or Bel will. Why?" I can't stop myself from asking. Maybe I haven't managed to shove the jealousy away completely.

"Of course they will." She starts towards the car and I finally allow the door to shut before following her. "I want to be able to call and check on Alyssa between now and Monday."

Pushing the button on my key fob, I unlock the car before she reaches for the handle. "Monday?"

"I told her I'd come back and see her on Monday, when the buses are running." She says buses like there's more than one. Mount Roxby has one bus that drives through the town over and over again. The driver's name is Simon. He does a good job, driving through most of the streets and not just the main ones on the route. But in saying that, it means the schedule never runs on time due to the detours.

"I'll drive you. No buses for you and your precious cargo." I nod towards her stomach. My hand itches to reach out and touch it, but I know some women hate random people touching their pregnant bellies and I'd rather not make her feel uncomfortable.

"Cain Wilson! Are you insinuating I'm as big as an aeroplane?" I flick my eyes off the road to see if she's joking with me. Her slack jaw and wide eyes have me anxious before she laughs. "Don't look so worried."

Fuck it. Biting the bullet, I reach out blindly—my eyes back on the road—and place my outspread palm on her beautiful bump. "This does not resemble an aeroplane in the slightest." I move my hand in a circular motion. The soft cotton of her summer dress is so thin I can feel the warmth of her skin through it. "I meant it earlier when I said you're beautiful. No one is as beautiful as you." I flick my eyes to her and catch her watching me.

She shakes her head. "I've seen plenty of women who are prettier than me. Frankie is for a start." Taking my hand off her stomach, I grab her hand in mine, entwining our fingers.

"Nobody holds a candle to you." Lifting her hand to my lips, I press a gentle kiss to her fingers.

I can see her observing me out the corner of my eye. "Did you two… date?" Before I get a chance to answer her question, she snatches her hand out of mine and speaks, once again. "Forget I asked. I have no right to ask that." She groans and rubs her face with her hands, obviously distressed about either her question or having asked it.

Flicking the indicator on, I pull to the side of the road. After putting the car in park, I unclip my seatbelt and turn my body to face her, as much as the seat and steering wheel allow me to.

Reaching out, I cup her cheek with one hand, feeling reassured as she leans into my touch. "You have every right to ask me." I take her hand in mine again and kiss it, needing to taste her. "I'm yours and I always will be, whether you want me or not."

She swallows what I can only assume is a lump in her throat. "Cain… I…."

I place a finger over her lips to stop her talking. "Don't. You don't have to say anything. Just know that I'm here for you, even if all you ever want is friendship. Okay?" I don't remove my finger to allow her to speak, so she nods in agreement.

Satisfied, I straighten in my seat, put the car in gear, and then pull out onto the empty street. "It was never like that between me and Frankie. I saved her from a living hell and kept her safe until she felt ready to tell me who she was. It took her a long time so we became close, but it was purely platonic." I push down my rising anger. It's anger that always rushes to the surface when I think of that hellhole she was in. "In any case, she was already mated. And so am I… technically." I shrug nonchalantly as I give her a quick smile. I don't want her to feel pressured into feeling things she may not be ready for.

10

PART OF THE PACK

*B*eing with Alyssa was hard. She's always been such a happy person, so seeing her so withdrawn really pulled on my heartstrings. She acknowledged my words with a nod, though whether she actually heard what I was saying is another thing entirely. I will go back though. She needs people, and considering she only wants to be with Jared because he's not pack, he's going to need a break every now and then. Having made the decision to go back, I let thoughts about Alyssa and Jared leave my mind as I watch the scenery fly by through the windscreen.

"I'm yours and I always will be, whether you want me or not." Cain's words are on repeat in my head as he drives us through the dark empty streets. Of course I want him. I just don't know if I can handle the heartbreak if it all goes wrong again. What if he's wrong about me being his mate and it all falls apart? Would he just turn around and say, "Sorry I was mistaken?" That would kill me now, let alone if I'd fallen for him even more. My stomach is in knots just thinking about it.

"Hey." Cain's hand brushes my knee. "Are you okay? You're really quiet and seem to have come over a little sad."

I look at the scenery out the window, seeing we're just turning into the large drive. "Yeah. I'm just thinking how cruel the world is. Wes was a nice guy, you know? He didn't deserve to die."

Cain pulls the car into a space beside Billy's bike and turns off the engine. "Good people never deserve to die, beautiful. Unfortunately, sometimes there's nothing that can be done to stop it."

Knowing he's right, I nod. "At least Alyssa and the baby have everyone here." I wave at the house as we walk up to the door. "You'll all help her through it, just like you did for me." Turning the handle, I walk into what's fast become my home once again. The house is still brimming with people. It seems like maybe even more have arrived since we left.

Wanting to get out of the way, I edge my way towards the corridor leading to my room. Billy stops in front of us, blocking my escape.

"How is she?" he asks. I frown, wondering how he even knows where we've been. "Theo told us you went to see her," he explains.

"She's pretty out of it, but Jared is taking good care of her." I try to give him a reassuring smile, but I know I fail. I just can't seem to smile after seeing her so broken.

He nods. "He's a good guy." He weighs me up with his eyes and grins. "Theo told us you know our secret too. Welcome to the pack." He pulls me into a hug and I come out of it feeling dazed. *Part of the pack?*

"I'm not part of the pack," I say, glancing at Cain. Do people know about what went on between me and Cain all those years ago? Surely Theo won't have announced that.

"You've always been part of the pack, sweetheart," Billy informs me, giving me a warm smile. "Ever since Theo brought you home." He shrugs. "You just know about it now."

"Oh." I let out a nervous giggle as my stomach settles. "Thank you. Although I'm pretty sure most people have hated me for most of that time, and especially since I left."

He waves a hand dismissing my words. "Not the important people." He throws me a wink before looking at Cain over my shoulder. "I also hear you're staying with us? Welcome back, buddy." I step aside as they have a manly hug. Making the most of their distraction, I slip off down the corridor and head to bed, wanting to get away from the grief that fills the room before it dredges up old memories.

Lying in the dark, I listen to the gentle chatter of the people below. Hearing the sound of car doors, I gather people must be finally heading to their own homes.

A knock on my bedroom door startles me into a sitting position.

"Mum. What are you doing?" I hear Cain's voice question Trudy through the door.

"I wanted to let Selena know she isn't the only one around here who isn't a werewolf," Trudy says, sounding somewhat excited at the prospect.

"I'm sure she'll be happy to hear that, but I'm fairly sure she's asleep. She looked pretty drained when we got back from Alyssa's. Why don't you tell her tomorrow?" Cain sounds anxious, and I can't help but wonder if I did look as drained as I felt. *God, I hope not.*

"Good idea." I hear a shuffling sound and assume they're walking away. "Wait a minute. Your room's at the other side of the house. Why were you up here?" Hearing Trudy's question has my heart pounding in anticipation of Cain's answer. I hold my breath to hear better.

"Like I said, she was drained. I just wanted to check she was okay. I can't hear her moving and the lights off, so she must be sleeping."

I release my breath, filled with disappointment at his explanation. *What was I expecting him to say?* I shake my head at my own stupidity.

"Come on. I'll make you a cuppa. I have a feeling you have a lot to fill me in on." Trudy's voice sounds quieter as their footfalls pad away.

Closing my eyes, it doesn't take me long to drift off into a dreamland that has Cain walking in and doing wicked things to me.

11.

IT'S THE HORMONES

SELENA

As usual I barely slept last night. I thought you lost out on sleep once the baby arrived and needed feeding through the night, not before. Looking at the bed after getting washed and dressed, I feel like I could just fall back into it and sleep for a week, but instead, I lean over and tug the covers straight. I know if I start napping throughout the day, I won't even get the couple of hours sleep at night that I'm currently getting. Plus, I'd planned on going to see Alyssa again today, even if it's just to give Jared a moment to catch his breath. There must be a lot of pressure on his shoulders. Yesterday I'd told him I'd return on Monday, but having thought about it overnight, I'm pretty certain he won't have had the time to go grocery shopping yet, and I want to give him the opportunity to do that because I don't think the idea has crossed anyone else's mind either.

Losing my father and brother would have killed me too if I hadn't had Cain. Theo may have gotten me through the months following the loss of my family, but Cain, he got me through those important first few hours. Even thinking back on it now, it's a fuzzy blur. I was so disconnected from everything, but his presence was like a warm blanket when I'd felt numb with cold.

Knocking on the door pulls me out of my memories. "One

sec," I call out as I grab my empty glass off the bedside cupboard, not wanting to have to come back up for it later—waddling up and down the stairs takes energy I don't seem to have these days.

Pulling the door open, the peppermint aroma of a steaming tea hits me as a cup is thrust in my face.

"Tea?" Trudy asks, seemingly full of energy if her dancing feet are anything to go by.

I sidestep her and place my hands around hers on the cup, aiming to calm her movements before the hot liquid can burn either of us. "Sure, thanks. Let me take that before you spill it." I glance at my watch to double-check the time. "How many coffees have you had this morning, Trudy?" Seven o'clock is way too early for her to be this jittery from coffee. Knowing she used to have a problem with drugs and alcohol causes worry to surge through me as I wonder if she's fallen off the wagon, again. I can't imagine what would have caused her to do such a thing. As far as I know, she wasn't close to Wes.

She waves me to lead the way downstairs, and I do just that, hoping once I have my back turned, she'll feel more comfort-able to talk. I've barely taken three steps when words tumble out of her mouth.

"I've had a couple. I couldn't sleep last night." She pauses, taking a deep breath. "I had hoped that you'd maybe be in the same boat. Actually no… I didn't want you not to be sleeping, but I really wanted to catch you down there like we often do during the night."

I stop at the bottom of the stairs and turn to face her. "Trudy, you're worrying me. Are you okay?" I peer at her, taking in her clean blouse and jeans. She doesn't look like she's been on a bender. Leaning forward slightly, I breathe in, aiming to get a discreet whiff of her breath.

"I haven't been drinking if that's what you're sniffing for," she says, making it perfectly clear I wasn't as discreet as I'd been aiming. "I didn't mean to worry you." She pats at her blonde bob. "Shall we go sit on the deck? You can drink your tea and I'll explain what's gotten me so excited."

I look at her full of surprise; my eyebrows must almost be in my hairline. "This is you excited?" She laughs and gives me a sheepish nod. "Okay, but I'll have to sit at the garden table because I won't get out of the lounger if I try to sit on that." I head through the French doors and pull a chair out at the table sitting on the edge of the grass.

As I wait for Trudy to be seated and tell me what's going on in that crazy head of hers, I glance around the yard, taking in the tables and chairs that had all been part of a wedding only a couple of days ago. All that happiness has been wiped away with death. Theo and Bel should be having a honeymoon, not planning the burial of a friend. A family member, that's what he was. Wes was as good as Theo's brother. I could see that, even before I knew about the pack connection.

"The wedding feels like weeks ago, but the flowers aren't even wilted." Trudy sighs, and I watch her finger the centre-piece between us. She shakes her head as if to clear it of whatever thoughts are present before grabbing my hand on the table and giving it a squeeze. "That's not what I wanted to talk about."

I wipe at a tear with my spare hand, my hormones clearly getting the better of me.

"I had a long chat with Cain last night. I want you to know you aren't the only human around here. I've always been an outsider of sorts." I frown, unsure where she's going with this, but I allow her to finish without interrupting with questions. "Don't get me wrong, you'd never be an outsider. Not if you mated with Cain."

I cough. "*Trudy!* I... we... I think you have the wrong end of the stick. Cain and I aren't—"

She cuts me off with a wave of her hand. "Oh, I know

exactly what's happening, but don't worry about that for now. What I'm trying to say is, I'm here if you need to talk to someone without the pack bonds and stuff, if they get pushy." She looks at me with raised eyebrows. "Because werewolves can be pushy bastards."

"*Mum!*" Cain's voice coming from the trees at the other side of the yard has me jumping in my seat. "I told you to leave her alone. Jesus, are you trying to scare her off?"

"I'll have you know I'm offering her support." The indignation in her voice makes me laugh.

Closing my eyes, I soak in the warmth of the sun as I listen to them bickering.

"You were calling us pushy bastards, Mum." Cain's voice sounds much closer than it had been a moment ago. The sound of a chair knocking the table alerts me to the fact he must be joining us.

Opening my eyes, I take a sip of the rapidly cooling peppermint tea whilst watching Cain over the top of the mug. He's giving his mother a stern look. I can tell he's only joking by the slight lift at the corner of his mouth. He has a slight shadow over his jaw, making me aware that he probably hasn't shaved this morning. I lift my hand, wanting to run my fingers over the scrub only to catch myself, tucking my own hair behind my ear in hopes of disguising my hand's initial intentions.

"You can be pushy," Trudy argues gently. "And you were born out of wedlock, so technically...." She grins, clearly thinking he won't argue with her reasoning.

"Well played, Mum." He laughs. The sound caresses my skin as I watch him pull her into a one-armed hug.

I'm surprised by her words. I knew she hadn't always been with Marcus, Cain's dad, because when I first started dating Theo, Marcus was with another woman, Margie. I had no idea they hadn't actually been married beforehand. Margie hated Cain and Theo and made it perfectly clear whenever she had the chance. Come to think of it, she hated me too. Thinking back on it now, I wonder if it was because I wasn't a werewolf.

"So, what do you ladies have planned for today?" He releases Trudy and flicks his eyes between the two of us. I look to Trudy.

She shrugs. "Nothing yet."

Both their eyes fall to me. "I was planning on visiting Alyssa again."

Cain glances at his watch. "If you give me twenty minutes, I can drop you off on my way to work and then I'll pick you up again when I finish around lunch."

"You're working?" I ask, my voice high with surprise.

"My brother owns a gym, which conveniently has a vacancy since Paddy left town," Cain says, before throwing me a wink. "You didn't think I was planning to be a slacker, did you?" Pushing his chair back, he stands.

"No, it's just… it was only yesterday you decided to stay in town." My heart beats erratically in my chest at the thought of him staying. We caused such a mess all those years ago, and here we are back in the same town. Hell, we're in the same house. "It was quick," I add.

"I, for one, am glad you're staying," Trudy exclaims with a gentle squeeze of his arm.

"Thanks, Mum." He leans and gives her a kiss on the cheek. "Now, I really do have to get ready for work. I'll meet you by the car in twenty?" He looks at me, his eyebrow raised in question.

I nod and watch as he runs into the house. His sweats and T-shirt cling to his muscles. Muscles that will have water running over them any second now. I lick my lips and shake my thoughts of him naked in the shower out of my head, before turning my attention back to Trudy, who is sporting the biggest, knowing grin. "Oh, shut up. It's the hormones," I admit guiltily.

Trudy purses her lips and a frown creases her brow. "Have you seen him in his other form?"

"Wolf?" I ask stupidly, as if there's another form of his.

She nods.

"No." I shake my head. "I didn't think they'd be allowed to change in front of us. I remember he said their existence is a big secret and it's dangerous for us to even know about it."

She reaches across the table and squeezes my hand. "You'll see them soon enough. It's magnificent." Without any more explanation, she heads off towards the house, leaving me wondering why they'd risk showing me if it's so dangerous.

Glancing at my own watch, I figure I have enough time to have a quick bathroom break before heading to the car.

I knock on the door before me as I listen to the car idling at the kerb. Cain's waiting to see that I get in safely. It's not like I'm a grown woman or anything.

Jared opens the door, looking somewhat bedraggled in a T-shirt and loose-fitting shorts. His hair's sticking out in all directions having seemingly just woken up. "Se—" He clears his throat before trying again. "Selena, I wasn't expecting you until Monday."

I grimace. I should have called. "I—"

"I'm being rude, forgive me." He rubs a hand over his face. "I just stumbled out of bed. Come in." He waves me in, and I have a quick glance out the door before he closes it, catching sight of Cain pulling onto the road. I step into the lounge and Jared follows. "Alyssa's still asleep. Do you want a coffee? Actually, I'm not sure if we have decaf."

"I'm assuming you haven't really had a chance to do any shopping. That's kind of why I came today." I frown, hoping he doesn't think I'm butting into their business. "I figured since

Alyssa was okay with me yesterday, you might like to pop out and grab what you want. Or if you don't fancy leaving, I can go pick some stuff up for you. Although I'd probably have to borrow your car." Sure I'm babbling, I press my lips together to stop myself from going on.

Jared strokes a hand down my arm, like I've seen the werewolves do a thousand times. "Hey, it's okay. It's really nice that you thought of doing that for me. I'd actually like to quickly pop to the shop for a few bits." He turns his head to the side as though he's listening to something before focusing back on me. "Come into the kitchen with me. We can get a list together while we wait for Alyssa to wake up. I don't want to leave without telling her first."

I smile. "Sure. That sounds like a good plan."

12

DIE TRYING

SELENA

$\mathcal{A}$s I make my way to the kitchen for my afternoon peppermint tea, there's a knock on the front door just as I'm passing. Reaching out, I open it and turn to let them in without much thought. It's a pack house after all; there are people coming and going all the time.

The face of the person standing at the door registers with my brain and my heart starts to race. "Stu," I whisper. I never thought I'd see him again, not after he all but booted me out the door when I told him I was pregnant. My hands drop to my stomach in a protective gesture, and his eyes follow their movement. I fell into Stu's lap—quite literally—within hours of leaving Mount Roxby. I'd stopped off in a tavern in the next town over and drank myself into a stupor, before falling over my feet and landing in his lap. Stu took me home with him. Even though over time, I felt he was keeping secrets from me just like Theo had, I ignored the little supernatural warning signs that should have had me running a mile, and I settled into life with Stu. It was amazing. He was a caring boyfriend, and I thought I could see us lasting the long haul. Until I told him I was pregnant. That's when he became a whole other person. *Violent.* Terrifyingly violent. I ran to Theo hoping for a second chance, but I also ran to Theo because I knew he'd protect me and my child. No matter what had happened between us in the past, he'd never put a child in danger.

"You haven't popped it out yet then." His stating of the obvious makes me glare at him, belatedly remembering how much he hated me glaring at him. He steps forward menacingly and pulls me out the door with a harsh grip on my arm that causes pain to radiate along the limb. "If you want to live long enough to have that baby, you better wipe that look off your face."

Falling back into old habits, I cower before him, dropping my eyes to the floor and slouching my shoulders. "I'm sorry."

"You better let go of her and leave." Cain's demanding voice behind me has me relaxing instantly. Stu can't do anything to harm me or my baby, not while Cain's here. "Right. The. Fuck. Now!" The growl behind Cain's words has the hairs on the back of my neck standing on end. Cain steps up beside me, and I glance at him gratefully as he brushes a reassuring hand over my back.

Stu releases my hand as he locks eyes with Cain. "I'll be going as soon as I've collected what belongs to me." The set of Stu's shoulders and his feet planted firmly where he stands shows how determined he is as he points to my stomach.

"I think you might be mistaken, mate, because she's *mine!*" The growl in that one word makes the hairs rise on the back of my neck.

"That baby she's carrying is *mine.* So, I'm taking her with me." Stu takes a step towards me, making his intentions perfectly clear.

Cain gently ushers me behind him. "You're not taking my mate anywhere, but you are more than welcome to die trying." Hearing Cain call me his mate has my heart skipping a beat. I rub a hand over my belly wondering if he really meant it and, if he did, has he considered that another man's baby comes with me?

"Mate? If I'd have known you knew about us, we could have had some real fun in the bedroom." He winks at me over

Cain's shoulder, making bile rise in my throat at his insinuation.

Cain lets out a furious growl and charges forward.

Suddenly overwhelmed with the need to protect Cain from getting hurt because of me, I jump forward, grabbing his arm. "Please," I plead. He turns his head to look at me. His eyes are glowing an ice-blue, reminding me of the wolf's eyes he once showed me.

Knowing I need to get Stu to leave, I turn my attention to him and I speak up. "You kicked me out the minute you found out I was pregnant. Why do you want it now?" I can feel Cain's skin beneath my fingers rippling, and I slide my hand down, taking his hand in mine, hoping to calm him. I've lived with wolves long enough to know touch like this is something that calms them.

"Honestly, I'd rather kill you both right now, but my alpha feels differently." Cain's hand tightens painfully on mine, causing me to grit my teeth.

"I'll tell you what." Cain words seem forced, as though it's taking all his energy to fight something else. "Go tell your alpha if he really wants my mate's child, he can come back when it hits puberty." He loosens his hold on my hand, and I quickly cradle it in my other hand, massaging it and hoping to get the blood flowing again. Stu grins seemingly satisfied. "Don't get me wrong, he won't be leaving with the child, but I'll be more than happy to end his life for him when he does come knocking."

Stu stares at Cain, indecision written in the crease of his brow. "Fucking rock and hard place, every fucking time," he mutters to himself.

"Now, if you don't want me to show you what being between a rock and a hard place really feels like, you might wanna get off my property... *NOW!*"

Turning without a word, Stu hightails it down the drive.

The speed he moves tells anyone watching that he's something other than human. I've never seen anyone move so fast

"Fucking arrogant fox, moving like that. Humans could be around for all he knows." Cain stares at the drive as if he can see through the trees Stu ran into.

"He's a fox?" My voice rises in surprise. Cain spins to face me and nods in answer. "I had no idea there were more than just werewolves."

"Any animal could be a were-animal or shifter as some prefer to be called. In fact…" He glances around as though looking for something, before training his eyes back on me. "Jared isn't a wolf. He's a lion."

My eyebrows almost pop out of my head with surprise, or so it feels anyway. "A lion? Like a big, roaring, golden-maned, lion?"

He nods and grins. "I haven't seen him in his lion form, so I can't say whether he's big or not. But considering he's meant to be his pride's next alpha, I'd assume he's pretty big."

"Oh wow, I'd love to see it. His lion. I bet he's so majestic." I wave my hands in excitement at the thought and hiss as pain soars through the one Cain had squeezed the life out of.

Cain's eyes drop to the offending appendage and his smile is wiped from his face. I pull the hand behind my back, trying to hide it from his view. "Selena, let me see it."

Not wanting him to see the bruise I'd caught sight of a second ago, I try to placate him. "It's nothing, just a little bruise."

"Please, Selena." The pleading and his solemn eyes have me moving my hand out from behind my back and placing it into his outstretched palm. I avert my eyes from his face, not quick enough to miss the anguish in his pained stare. "That was me, wasn't it?" His grim look tells me he already knows the answer. "I'm sorry… I…. *Fuck!* There's no excuse for something like this. I know you're human. How could I have done this?"

Taking my hand out of his, I fight not to show the discomfort the movement causes as I cup his face. "Cain. Listen to me. It wasn't your fault." He opens his mouth to argue, but I rush to keep talking, not giving him the chance to jump in. "I knew your wolf was close to the surface. I saw him in your eyes and felt your skin rippling under my fingers. *I* put my hand in yours anyway. It was my fault. Not yours."

He turns his face to kiss the bruised hand. "You need an X-ray."

I sigh as I give him a short, sharp nod. I'd come to the same conclusion the second it happened.

He pulls his phone out of his pocket as I drop my hands from his face and cradle them over my stomach. "Zainab," he says, holding the phone out in front of him, having put it on speaker. "I need your expertise."

"Okay," Zainab's voice answers warily through the speakers.

"Is there still an X-ray machine in the big shed?"

"Yes. Why? What have you done?" Her voice sounds anxious, no doubt at the thought of someone hurt.

"Selena has hurt her hand. It's bruised up pretty quickly, so it looks like there could be a fracture or two." He grimaces with the words, and I offer him a reassuring smile, trying to show him I'm okay.

"Selena? No, the baby… we don't have a lead apron, so she can't have an X-ray in the shed."

"Fuck."

"Cain, it's probably just a bruise. Don't worry about it. A bit of ice and a couple of days and it'll be on the mend." I reach out, trying to soothe him with touch again, but he steps back before our skin connects.

"I am worried about it, Selena. You're in pain. I can sense it. And It's my fucking fault."

"Cain!" Zainab's voice shouts through the phone's speakers, reminding us both that she's still present and listening to every

word. "Are you listening to me now?" He lets out a rumble "I'll take that as a yes." My eyes widen in surprise as I realise Zainab heard the sound. "My shift is nearly over. I can borrow an apron from work and do the X-ray when I get there. Is that okay with you both?"

"Thanks, Zainab." The defeat in Cain's voice pulls at my heart.

"It's what I'm here for. I'll see you both soon," she says before hanging up.

Cain shoves his phone back in his pocket, and I do the only thing I can that will pull him out of his own head.

I kiss him.

Kiss him with everything I have.

Kiss him like I've imagined kissing him for the longest time.

Fisting my hands in his shirt, I tug him down towards me so I don't have to balance on my tiptoes.

It doesn't take him long to reciprocate. One of his hands slips around my waist as the other slides across my neck and grips the hair at my nape. His mouth moves on mine ferociously, like he's drinking me in.

We finally break apart, both breathing heavily, staying wrapped up in each other as close as my gigantic belly will allow. "Selena, does that mean—"

I answer before he even finishes his sentence. "Yes, Cain. You said it yourself." I dive in for a quick peck on his lips, just because I can. "I'm yours… your mate."

He drops to his knees and holds my enormous belly between his hands. "Did you hear that in there? Your mummy just said she's mine." Like magic the baby gives a kick in answer, causing Cain to look up at me in awe. "You like the sound of that, too, don't you?" he says, once again focusing his attention on my belly.

"Of course, it does. Because that means it's going get the most wonderful daddy by default." I laugh at the warmth of his breath as he kisses my bump through the thin fabric of my top.

He reluctantly gets to his feet, his movements slow. "Let's go get you some ice and wait for Zainab in the shed. Once you've had the X-ray, I can spend the rest of the day revelling in your body." It feels like a swarm of butterflies are floating around in my stomach as I take in his words. It's been such a long time since we've been together like he's suggesting. As much as I want nothing more than for us both to take pleasure in each other's nakedness, what if he's disappointed in what he finds beneath my clothes? My body isn't what it once was.

***

*W*e walk into the shed, and I marvel at the sight before me. The floor is covered in those foam mats that you'd find in a martial arts place, not that I've seen any real-life martial arts places. I've seen them in the movies though, so I'm sure that's what they must look like.

Along the back wall of the shed, there are what look like hospital beds—three of them all lined up. *Do these guys get that many injuries that they'd need three all at once?* I ask as much. "Do you really need three hospital beds?" I glance at Cain over my shoulder, wanting to see his face as he answers.

"Being a werewolf has its dangers." He shrugs. "And it's not like we can go down to the hospital. We heal too quickly, so we'd draw unwanted attention."

I nod, understanding his reasoning.

A woman of Indian decent walks into the shed, something black with maroon piping hanging over her arm. "Selena, it's nice to finally meet you. I've been in the pack since before you and Theo, but I don't think we've ever met." She looks at me, an eyebrow raised quizzically.

She doesn't look familiar at all. "I don't think we've met

before." I shrug, unsure. "But my memory is rubbish, so I could be wrong."

She laughs. "That will be the baby brain. It only gets worse once the baby arrives."

"You've got kids?" I ask, surprised. I hadn't noticed any kids in the time I've been around Theo and the pack, except Alyssa. I assumed they struggled to have children.

"I was bitten and had my first shift after I had kids," she states with a knowing nod, before wheeling a stool over to one of the beds. She positions a plastic board with grid type markings on top of the bed, before motioning for us to join her. She hands me the apron, which is far heavier than she made it look. "If you just put your arms in here." I do as instructed and glance at Cain, who's leaning against the wall beside the bed. His leg's bent at the knee, his foot flat against the wall.

He gives me a reassuring smile, before I look back to Zainab as she tells me how to position my hand for the X-ray.

"That's perfect," she says, once she has me sat on the stool with my hand outspread on the plastic board. She pushes a button on the machine and repositions my hand before doing it again, my hand at a slightly different angle. "That should be enough."

We head over to a computer in the corner of the room, which I'd not noticed on entering the shed. After Zainab clicks the mouse a few times, an X-ray of a hand pops onto the screen. My hand.

I squint at the screen, trying to see a break of some kind jumping out at me. Deciding there's nothing obvious to me, I turn to watch Zainab's face. She is the qualified doctor after all.

Zainab's lips are pressed together as she frowns at the screen, clicking through the different shots of my hand. "Okay. Do you see here?" She points at the screen. "That mark there is a fracture." She points elsewhere on the screen. "As is that."

Cain stiffens beside me and I grab his hand with my good

one, praying to whatever god wants to listen. *Please let that be it*.

Zainab changes the screen to one of the other images and points at the screen again, making my heart sink. "There is another."

Cain growls, and I squeeze his hand, trying to comfort him. He snatches his hand back and paces behind us. I don't know what he's doing, but whatever it is has the hairs on the back of my neck standing to attention, and a shiver runs down my spine.

Zainab takes a deep breath before speaking again, sounding somewhat pained. "Luckily, they're just fractures so you won't need surgery, just a cast."

I nod, before turning my attention back to Cain. I take a tentative step towards him until Zainab reaches out, halting my steps with a hand on my arm.

"Give him a minute," she says, her tone demanding.

"He's blaming himself," I say, my voice high-pitched, unable to keep a lid on my anxiety. I need to help him.

"He *can* hear you, you know?" The deepness of his voice tells me he's anything but calm.

I pull my arm out of Zainab's hold.

"Be careful, Selena. His wolf is riding him right now. I can feel it," Zainab warns, whilst rubbing her hands over her forearms.

I take slow, sure steps towards him, wanting to show them both that I'm not scared of Cain, or his wolf. I know neither of them will do anything to harm me again. He's punishing himself too much for his earlier mistake.

"Cain," I say as I approach him, not wanting to startle him. I place my hand firmly on his broad back as I step around him, sliding my hand over his shoulder and down his arm as I go.

He stands stock still, and I worry he might shrug me off. I stop before him and look up into his eyes.

Ice-blue eyes.

Not Cain's eyes.

His wolf's.

"Mate." The word leaves my mouth before it even registers in my head. I have no idea what it means—the fact that I've said it—but I know it's momentous.

Zainab makes a noise behind me, but I'm too focused on Cain and his wolf to pay attention to her.

Cain swallows. "Mate." His voice is deeper and gruffer than usual. It's the voice of his wolf. His hand snakes out and slides roughly around the back of my neck. Pulling me close to him, forceful, but without hurting me.

My eyes are locked on his wolf's eyes.

He leans forward and I think he's going to kiss me, but his mouth brushes past my jaw before he bites at my neck.

I gasp in shock at his move and the slight pain it causes.

He licks and kisses the spot, like he's caressing it, causing me to giggle as I grip at his bicep with my good hand. My knees start to give and my body floods with my arousal as he slowly kisses his way back up my jaw, to my lips.

I close my eyes, luxuriating in the feel of his warm mouth on me, imagining it being in other places. Places that are now tingling with need.

His mouth disappears, and I take a few seconds to compose myself before I open my eyes. I'm greeted with happiness beaming out of Cain's deep blue eyes, his smile wide across his face.

"Hey," he says, his voice sounding like his once again.

"Hey," I say with a grin of my own. "Mate," I add, letting him know, I understand the depth of what just happened between us.

We claimed each other. *Permanently.* Whether there are more steps to the claiming—if that's even what it's called—or not, there's no going back from what we've just done.

And I for one, wouldn't want there to be.

13.

MINE AT LAST

CAIN

My wolf settles down, content in finally having our mate accept us. We've been waiting for it for such a long time. I search her blue eyes, wondering if really understands what just happened between us. The confidence I see tells me she does.

Unable to wipe the smile off my face, I crush my lips on hers as I hold her body against mine. Running my hands over her curves, excitement fills me as I think about being able to trace these curves with my mouth.

A throat clears behind us, and I get pulled back to reality and the shed.

"If you'd like to be left alone to…" Zainab clears her throat again. "Finish what you've started, you need to let me put a cast on that hand."

Her hand. My euphoria comes crashing down. I fractured Selena's hand in numerous places. I broke my mate. How could I have been so rough?

A finger caresses my temple, and lips press a gentle kiss on the tip of my nose. "Please don't blame yourself, Cain. Watching you blame yourself hurts me more than the damn hand does."

Taking a deep breath, I'm almost floored by the scent of our arousal being so thick in the air. I immediately understand why

Zainab may have felt uncomfortable. I give Selena a reassuring smile as I try to push my self-blame back. "Let's get you patched up."

---

*I*t doesn't take Zainab long to fix a cast up. I don't know how she had all the equipment since we very rarely need casts due to our exceptionally quick healing abilities. Usually, we'll just strap anything broken in place whilst it fuses together.

"Six weeks? I need to keep this thing on for six weeks?" Selena glares at the stark white cast that covers her hand and most of her forearm. "I'm due in six weeks. What if the baby comes early? I won't be able to change nappies or anything." She shakes her head defiantly as she pulls at the opening around her fingertips. "Nope. Take it off. I can't have a cast."

I step up to her and place a calming hand on hers, hoping to still it. "Hey, calm down, beautiful. You don't want to cause more damage and have to have it on longer." I glance across at Zainab, pleading with my eyes for her to back me up.

"Yes." Zainab nods. "How about we play it by ear. We'll give you a weekly X-ray and reassess the situation as we see how it's healing. You could have it off in as soon as four weeks."

Zainab's words cause Selena to pause her ministrations. "Really?" She looks at Zainab, her eyes wary. "Four weeks?"

"Four weeks," Zainab reassures her with a wide smile, causing Selena to flash a smile back. I suddenly have the urge to hug the woman. She managed to talk Selena down from her panic, something I couldn't do. Part of me feels put out by that thought, but I brush it aside.

I pull Selena into my arms and press a kiss to her forehead. "How about we call for some takeaway and watch a movie or two?" I offer, wanting to take her mind off her worries. As much as I want to get her naked in my bed, I want it to happen for the right reasons, and as a distraction from her injury wouldn't be it.

She nods against my chest. "That sounds perfect."

I release my hold on her and pat her behind gently. "You go pick the food and the movie, and I'll help Zainab clean up here. I'll be with you in five."

Zainab waves me off. "Don't worry about it. I know exactly where everything belongs. It will take me twice as long to clean up if I'm telling you where to put everything. Go, enjoy your night."

Selena steps forward and says thank you to Zainab, giving her a quick hug before heading back to the house.

Bending slightly, I place a gentle kiss on Zainab's cheek. "Thanks. For everything."

She waves me off once again. "Go, enjoy your mate, before I change my mind and make you clean up the mess."

I laugh and back out of the shed with my arms raised in surrender.

I find Selena in the kitchen, flicking through a handful of takeaway menus. Picking two out of the pile, she holds them up, fanned out in her good hand. "Chinese or Indian?"

The thought of honey chicken and sweet and sour pork has my taste buds singing. "Chinese," I answer instantly.

As Selena states her choice. "Indian."

I laugh and surrender the choice to her. "Indian sounds great. Pick what you want and I'll give them a call."

She hands me the menu without looking at it. "Butter chicken and garlic naan bread."

I shake my head in disbelief. "You'd already decided before you even gave me the option." I laugh. "Did you just want to torture me with the thought of Chinese food?" I take the menu and pretend to pout.

She lets out a chuckle, clearly amused with my silly pouting face. "I didn't, honestly. I always have the same thing when I have a curry." She frowns and I want to rub away the crease between her eyes. "In fact, I'm pretty boring. I have one set meal from each of the takeaways. I never really have to look at a menu."

Taking note of the phone number, I throw the menu on the counter behind her before pulling her into my arms and taking her lips with mine. I want to wipe the frown off her face. She's anything but boring. Her body relaxes into mine within seconds of our lips connecting, and I contemplate ignoring the whole idea of food, to just sweep her up and take her to have my wicked way with her. The grumbling sound coming from her stomach has me pulling away with a laugh. "And on that note…" I release her and grab the phone out of the cradle on the side. "I better order some food."

In no time, I'm throwing the phone on to the counter and pulling Selena back into my arms. I can't seem to keep my hands off her. "Food should be here in twenty minutes. How do you want to pass the time?" I slide my hands down her back and over her perfect butt, giving it a gentle squeeze in the hope of hinting at what I'd like to do with the time we have.

She grins, raising a brow in a knowing look. "If we pass the time how you're thinking, we won't get fed at all because you won't be ready to stop at twenty minutes."

I roll my eyes playfully. "Fiiiine," I concede, knowing she's right. It'll take me all night to worship her how I want to. Twenty minutes just won't cut it. I tap her butt gently as I step away from her. "You go choose a movie and I'll grab us some drinks and plates for the food."

I potter around in the kitchen, keeping myself away from the temptation of Selena. The sound of a car on the gravel drive alerts me to the arrival of our takeaway. It reminds me of old times when I was avoiding her so I wasn't tempted to sleep with my brother's wife. Thank fuck those days are over and I only have to wait for another couple of hours.

I promised her food and a movie, and that's what she'll get —until I can finally make her mine.

It doesn't take me long to have everything served up. Placing Selena's glass of apple juice on the coffee table, I hand her the plate of food and watch as she balances it slightly on her stomach, causing me to let out a laugh.

"What?" She looks at me with wide, innocent eyes. "I have to reap some benefits from being this huge." Grabbing a piece of naan bread and popping it in her mouth, effectively stops her from explaining any further.

After collecting my own meal, I sit beside her, placing my beer on the coffee table before tucking into my lamb rogan josh. "What movie did you pick?" I ask between mouthfuls. She grins at me, and I wonder if she's going to torture me with a chick flick. "It's not *Bridget Jones*, is it?"

She laughs heartily, the sound causing my jeans to get tighter over my growing erection. "No, although I'm sure you enjoyed Bridget when I picked it for movie night once."

I purse my lips as I make a show of thinking. "Nope, I never paid attention to any of those movies. All I could think about was the feel of your feet pressing into the side of my thigh." Her wide-eyed expression makes me lose the joke in my voice and keeps me talking. "The three of us would share the couch, and although you'd be leaning against Theo, your feet would be encroaching into my seat. I loved it, and hated it in the same breath because even though I could feel the heat of your skin against mine, it reminded me I was never going to hold you in my arms like Theo did." Feeling raw and exposed, I swallow the lump rising in my throat.

"You were wrong, Cain. I'm yours. You can hold me whenever you want and nothing will ever change that." Her words sound like a promise.

I force myself to keep eating as I push my wolf down. He's trying to rush forward to claim her here and now.

Her eyes flick to mine, and I know she can see him in them. *"Yours."* That one word has him retreating without a fight.

Sitting on the couch with one leg across the back of it, I direct Selena to sit in the V of my legs. Her back against my chest.

"I'm heavy. I might crush you," she says with a wary look.

I give her a raised brow. "Get your mighty fine butt on this seat, or I'll have to skip the movie and carry you to bed to show you how heavy you aren't."

She lets out a sweet giggle before sitting exactly where I'd suggested. "Don't say I didn't warn you." She leans back without any hesitation, resting her head against my shoulder as I wrap my arms around her waist, placing them on her beautiful bump.

I give the top of her head a quick kiss before pressing Play on the remote and once again settling my hands across her bump. I mindlessly caress it as the movie starts, letting out a loud laugh as I realise what movie it is. "I should have guessed. You always loved Sandra Bullock movies." She would watch *Miss Congeniality* over and over again. The pack hated it. In fact, I think someone even went as far as throwing the DVD out after the fifteenth viewing.

"I couldn't find *Miss Congeniality*. So I chose the next best thing. *Heat*." Hearing the smile in her voice has one creeping across my own face as I settle back to enjoy the movie with my mate in my arms.

14.

CLAIM ME

SELENA

*C*ain's breath hitches against my ear as the baby wakes up and performs a somersault against Cain's hand, which has been resting on my bump rubbing circles here and there throughout the movie. The menu comes on the screen having run through the credits. I ignore it as I place my good hand over Cain's.

"Holy shit… it felt like she just rolled right over."

I laugh at the excitement in his voice. "*He* did." Butterflies flutter in my stomach at the thought of whether it could be a boy or a girl. There's a kick against the tip of Cain's finger, and he slides his palm over the spot.

"I can't imagine there'd be enough room for that. Wow." The awe in his voice keeps me lying there and allowing his hands to chase the baby's limbs as it moves around in it's little home.

The minutes pass and the movements start to become further apart and much gentler. "I think it's worn itself out. Or at least gotten comfortable," I say.

"Hmm. Well, I wonder what I should do with my hands now?" Cain asks, his voice gruff in my ear as one hand roams lower. Fingers brush under the edge of my underwear.

I let out a moan as I slip my hands behind his neck, awkwardly pulling him towards me with my casted arm so I can nuzzle at his throat.

His fingers rub over my sex and my core clenches. "Fuck, you're so responsive." He dips a finger inside as he rubs at my clit. The fingers on his other hand pinch at my nipple. His mouth descends on mine before he kisses his way down my jaw. The sensation of him being everywhere causes an orgasm to crash over me. He removes his hand from my underwear and I capture it in mine, tugging it back, greedy for more.

"*Please,* Cain."

"Shh. I'm not finished with you yet." His lips brush over my temple. "I just want to get you somewhere more comfortable." He manages to sit me up and eases out from behind me. He stands, and I move to slide my legs around so I can join him, only to be blocked as he bends and effortlessly scoops me into his arms.

"Cain, put me down." I push at his shoulders, trying not to be too hard with the heavy cast. "I'm too heavy for you to carry me."

Picking up his pace, he takes sure strides to his bedroom. "It's not my strength that will be in question if I drop you. It's your wriggling, so stop it."

Realising he's probably right, I pause my fidgeting and make the most of my position as I kiss my way up his jaw. My nibbling at his earlobe entices a growl from him.

"That's not exactly helpful either." He picks up his pace, and I struggle to track the things we pass, which tells me he's most probably tapping into his supernatural power. I'd seen Stu run this fast, but I'd never imagined I'd be able to experience it like this.

His door makes a loud bang as it hits the wall with force. It doesn't have the chance to hit us as it rebounds because I'm suddenly laid out on the bed with Cain standing over me. The heat in his eyes has me squirming in anticipation.

Remembering how he'd made me feel downstairs, I pull at

my stretchy maternity pants as I try to get naked. "Cain, I need you."

Cain stills my hands with his. "Let me." His hands taking over the job and he deftly removes my underwear and pants all in one gentle tug. Moving onto my top, he starts undoing the buttons one by one, and I curse myself for choosing to wear something so hard to take off. Having worked his way through the buttons, he peels the two sides open and runs a finger over the edge of my bra. I cringe internally as I picture the unflattering maternity bra I put on this morning. But the way Cain is looking at me wipes my thoughts away. He's looking at me as if I'm wearing the sexiest lace money could buy. He licks his lips before his head dips, and the feel of his warm, wet tongue traces the same path his finger had just been on. My eyes close in ecstasy. "Honeysuckle... mmm... I've missed the taste of you."

I arch my back to get closer to Cain just as his hands snake underneath me. The pressure of my bra releases and his fingers brush over my chest as he lifts the bra before finding a nipple with his mouth.

"I need you, Cain," I beg once again. "My hormones have made me so sensitive. *Please*...." I sit up as he helps me out of my bra and top.

Reaching for his jeans, I work on freeing him from their confines with the zipper and button.

"Selena." He breathes my name like a caress, sending goosebumps down my arms. "I—"

I kiss the rest of his sentence away as I shove his jeans and boxers down his legs. I wasn't kidding when I said I needed him.

The warmth of Cain's body follows me as I lie back on the bed. I wrap my legs around his waist, making our bodies come together where I need him most. "Cain...." I rub myself against him wantonly, hoping he catches on to what I'm aiming for because words are failing me.

He pauses and pulls back enough that our groins are no longer touching. I lock my legs around his waist to stop him from leaving completely. "Honey, I can't... the baby."

I frown as I lock eyes with him, seeing the concern etched into his face. My mind tries to make sense of his words. *The baby... what about the baby?*

"The baby won't care," I say, tugging at his arms as I try to pull us together again, but he's like a statue, solid and unrelenting. "It will be fine. Pregnant women have sex all the time."

I slide my hand between us and try to direct him to where he needs to be, only for him to pull away another inch.

"I swear to God, if you don't fuck me...." I let the sentence fall short, the threat to find someone else is on the tip of my tongue, but I daren't say it. If I say it and he can't follow through, I wouldn't want to find someone else. I open my mouth and say the only thing that I know will get him to past his irrational thoughts of harming the baby.

"Claim me, Cain."

15.

PACK MAGIC

CAIN

I twirl a strand of blonde hair around my finger, watching the sun shimmer through it. It looks like spun gold.

"Look, that one looks like a wolf." Selena's excited voice tears my eyes away from her hair and up at the sky.

We'd woken up at dawn—Selena unable to sleep because of the baby tap dancing on her bladder, and I wasn't willing to sleep when she couldn't—and decided to lay in the garden, to watch the stars go to bed as the sun rose through the trees surrounding the property.

A good hour passes by and Selena's guessing shapes of the clouds. I look where her finger is pointing and laugh.

"That looks more like an elephant. The ears are massive. Do you even know what a wolf looks like?" Her sudden silence makes me run over my words in my head. What the hell did I say that would take away her excitement so suddenly? All the other clouds we'd disagreed over, she'd laugh and insist she was right before moving onto the next one.

She turns her head to look at me as I change my position to lie on my side. Our new mate bonds tell me she's nervous, but I'm so used to reading her face I need to watch it now. "Actually, I've never seen a wolf. Well, only on TV." The look in her eyes is demanding. Does she really want what I think she does?

"Do you want to see one?" I ask tentatively. All the while, running names through my head of who I would be able to have change before her. It would have to be a submissive wolf. I wouldn't want a dominant wolf changing around her in case she spooks them or makes them see her as prey.

She shakes her head. "Not just any wolf, Cain. I want to meet your wolf."

I swallow as my wolf perks his ears, jumping to attention in that deeply hidden place he lives when I'm not in his form. "I... I'd never forgive myself if he hurt you."

She lifts her good hand and caresses my jaw with her palm. "He would never hurt his mate." Her hand slides down my neck and rests over my heart.

I place my hand over hers and feel my wolf come forward, knowing the eyes she can see in my face are his ice-blue ones. *"Never,"* my wolf says.

She rewards us with a heart-warming smile before pushing herself up and taking my lips with hers. Conscious of the strain it must cause her to be in that position, without breaking the kiss, I lower myself, so her head is once again resting on the ground.

I pull away, leaving us both panting for breath. I'd love to worship her body like I had last night, but not here in the garden where anyone could walk up on us.

Theo and Bel had stayed at a hotel last night, wanting some privacy from the pack, so we'd been lucky to have the privacy ourselves. Mum had stayed at Chloe's to give us space, and I'm assuming someone must have spoken to the rest of the pack because it's not often a night will go by without a pack member dropping by. Someone is bound to arrive home soon.

"Well then, I guess we should give our mate what she wants," I say, not quite sure whether I'm addressing her or my wolf. Maybe both. Standing, I start undressing, discarding my shirt on the floor as I bend slightly to tug down my jeans.

"Do you have to be naked to change?" she asks, her curiosity showing in the higher than normal pitch of her voice.

Fully naked, I throw my jeans on my shirt and glance down at her, my hands on my hips. "We don't have to be naked, but it's much more uncomfortable with clothes on. Not to mention, you ruin a lot of clothes if you shift in them."

Her gaze moving to my groin has it suddenly springing to attention under her scrutiny. Her tongue sneaks out to lick her lips, and I clear my throat, causing a blush to flow over her face at being caught ogling my dick. The sight makes me throw my head back and groan as I cover myself with my hand. "If you don't stop looking at me like that, you won't get to meet my wolf today. He'll force me to take you right here and now."

Her eyes suddenly pop up to meet mine. "How do you all manage to be naked in front of each other without, you know?" She nods in the direction of my dick while fighting to keep her eyes on mine.

"What, without jumping each other?" She nods, and I let out a laugh. "Nakedness isn't sexual for us. Not when we're doing it to shift. It's a necessity."

Selena frowns, and I feel like bending down to rub the cute crease between her brows away. I can't though, because I'll be too close to her and I'll want to do other things.

"So, you don't get turned on seeing the female wolves naked?" she asks.

Suddenly realising she may be feeling insecure about the female wolves, I grab my boxers and slide them back on. "I want to sit with you while we talk about this and I need clothes on to do that," I say, answering her questioning look.

Once beside her, I rub a hand over her beautiful bump as I let the words form on my tongue. "Like I said, being naked is a necessity to shift. It's just natural. Over time my eyes have learnt to avert themselves and I barely even notice they're naked. Obviously teenage guys are constantly getting wood, so seeing the females naked was a definite an issue during puberty." She nods, but I can tell she still has reservations by the sharpness of it and absence of even a small smile. "We try not to be naked in front of each other out of respect for mates, but sometimes it can't be avoided. I promise you, I have never had a female wolf look at me full of lust like you just did."

"Really?" she asks, her eyes wide in disbelief. "They must be blind… or crazy." She presses her lips against mine before pulling away all too quickly. Missing her mouth on mine, I try to connect our lips again only to have her lean back out of reach. "Nope. No more kissing until I've met your wolf."

With a roll of my eyes, I stand up and remove my boxers once again. "You are such a fun spoiler."

"Fun spoiler?" She lets out a giggle. "I'm not spoiling. I'm just postponing."

Silence falls over us as I crouch and allow my wolf to come forward. My shift doesn't take long. Ever since I defeated my dad—my alpha—my shift has been quick. It's still painful, but it's something I can handle. I'd expected my shift speed to revert to a slower pace once I handed the pack to Theo, since most alphas can use the power of the pack to speed up their shift, but it never did. Maybe it was a perk of defeating my alpha. Who knows? I guess it's just another mystery of the werewolf to add to the list of mysteries we seem to carry.

I shake out the last tingles of the change and let out a sneeze as my nose deals with the assault of all the extra scents it's picking up. I say *I,* but I can't help but wonder whether I should say my wolf since he's the one at the forefront. He never has complete control of my body, even when I'm in his form. It would be too dangerous; he's a predator and wouldn't think twice about taking someone down if he felt threatened. He needs my humanity to hold him back from running on instinct. If I left it to him, I'd probably end up lost in his form forever because he feels weak as a human, without his claws and teeth, so he'd never shift back.

Selena's gasp catches his attention. Lifting his head marginally, he takes the sight of her in. We both see the awe shining in her eyes, but he only knows what it is because I do. She looks different as I look out of his eyes, but her scent is the same. If not more intoxicating. He growls appreciatively as we breathe it in, before slowly padding towards her.

She doesn't move.

If it wasn't for the fact that I can't scent any fear, I'd guess her to be scared. I nudge my snout against her hand, hoping to ease any anxiety she may be feeling.

"You're beautiful," she states as she runs her fingers up my snout and over my head. I lay beside her, allowing her to play her fingers through my fur as she wishes, closing my eyes and basking the sensation. "You like that, huh?" She eases back down, still trailing her hand through my fur, and I'm aware we're resting just as we had been before I shifted.

The sound of an engine nearing has my eyes popping open and my muscles tensing, ready to attack if the visitor is an unwelcome one.

Selena's breathing beside me is steady and as I glance at her, I see she's fallen asleep. Going by the sun's position in the sky, it doesn't look to have moved a great deal, so not much time could have passed since we'd lain down.

The patio door slides open and I wait for our visitor to announce himself. Two distinct sets of footsteps on the decking tells me it's not one person like I'd thought. My wolf releases a warning growl before I can even try to use my other senses to identify them.

"Hey, that's no way to welcome us back from our extremely

short honeymoon." Theo's voice has us relaxing. There's no threat; it's just my idiot brother. I had been expecting him back today, so I don't know why we'd been on edge in the first place. My wolf growls at my thoughts. Making me grasp exactly why I was on edge. My pregnant mate is beside us, and all his protective instincts are kicking in full force, for her and our young.

Selena stirs beside us as I reposition myself to get a clear view of Theo and Bel. "Cain?" Her hand sinks into my fur. "You're still… I thought I heard voices."

"You did," Bel says, causing Selena to suddenly push up into a sitting position. I glare at Bel for making Selena jump, and Theo returns my growl.

"Don't growl at my mate."

"I wouldn't need to growl if she didn't scare my *mate."* I think towards him, forgetting not all wolves can communicate telepathically and especially out of wolf form. I'd hung around Frankie for too long. She was wolf born and had the gift of communicating telepathically with wolves, regardless of her form.

"That wasn't her intention. And besides, you know as well as I do that she isn't scared. There's no scent of fear." I lift my head, surprised he'd heard my thoughts. An amused grin spreads across his face. "What good is it to have a beta if I can't communicate with his wolf?"

"It's not official."

"You would have been my beta a long time ago if shit hadn't gone pear-shaped. Maybe being official in our hearts is enough for the pack magic." Bel takes Theo's hand in hers before giving it a comforting squeeze, obviously hearing something in his voice that I didn't. All alphas can communicate with their pack mates in wolf form, and their betas can communicate back. Some alphas have enough power that their whole packs can communicate in wolf form. Unfortunately, we aren't one of those packs. The only one I'm aware of is the Rossi Pack over in Western Australia.

Feeling the need to communicate properly, I stretch as I stand, readying myself to shift again. Grabbing my clothes between my teeth, I head for the trees at the edge of the garden. "What's happening?" I hear Selena ask as I trot through enough trees to give myself some cover as I change.

"He's shifting back," Theo explains.

"But why is he going away to do it?" Selena's confusion comes clear through our new mate bond, and I pause, ready to shift now to explain my reasons.

Theo takes over, obviously reading my mind again. "He didn't want you to feel uncomfortable about him being naked in front of Bel." The love that pours through our bond tells me I did the right thing. I push my love back through to her, hoping she can feel it as well as I can, even though she's human. We haven't had the chance to really learn what she can and can't feel through the bond. I don't know many mated humans. I should have asked Kelly when I was with the Rossi Pack. His mate was human. Although, she's no longer with him and I'm sure my mentioning her loss would only cause pain for him.

The shift comes over me as quickly, as it had earlier, and I'm pulling my clothes on in no time. I grit my teeth at the sensitivity of my skin as the material brushes against it, feeling like sandpaper.

I walk through the line of trees, my eyes falling immediately on Selena. She's struggling to stand, a hand on the floor and her belly almost up in the air. I run over. "Let me help," I offer, placing a hand under her armpits and lifting her with ease.

Once on two feet, she throws her arms around my neck, her baby bump pushing into me adorably. "Thank you."

I place a kiss on her temple. "I'm sure Theo or Bel would have helped you up if I hadn't got here first."

"Not for that, silly." She gives me a knowing look; she's

talking about my shifting under the cover of the trees. Maybe she didn't feel me through the bond after all.

"As much as this was nice and all"—Theo ruins our moment —"we need to chat business for a bit."

I give Selena an apologetic smile. "It looks like I need to earn my beta badge."

Bel clears her throat. "I was planning on going to spend some time with Misty. Would you like to come?" she offers, referring to her boss and friend. I can tell by the way Selena stiffens in my arms, she's going to decline the offer. "I'd love to get to know you better, Selena."

Selena snaps her head around to face Bel, probably in the hopes of trying to see if there's any truth to her words. I don't know what she sees, but she relaxes in my arms and nods. "I'd like that. Thank you."

"Great," Bel sounds genuinely happy about Selena's reply and even though I hadn't felt a lie, I realise she really meant what she'd said. I watch as she pulls my brother towards her, his shirt fisted in her hands.

His appreciative growl has me laughing. "Come on, guys. You do have an audience you know?"

Selena taps my arm gently. "Leave them alone. They're newlyweds."

I lean into her and let my arms slide down her sides. "We're newly mated. Does that mean I can get carried away with you not caring about our audience?"

"Mated?" Bel appears at my elbow and tugs Selena away from me. "You'll have to tell me all about that, but right now we need to leave or they'll never get to discussing pack business."

The sound of Selena's laughter is music to my ears as it fades away with every step she takes. I'm thankful for the effort Bel is making to get to know Selena. Having your true mate's estranged wife turn up acting like a mighty bitch and wanting him back, can't have been easy for her. Selena's personality change and willingness to sign the divorce papers probably went a long way to help though. As they round the side of the house, heading towards the car, Theo claps me on the back. "Come on then, brother. Let's deal with our responsibilities for a bit." He leads the way to the house, and I follow, planning to grab a beer on the way. "If we do it quickly, we might be able to meet the girls at the bar."

I pause midstride. "Misty's? Will Selena even be able to go in? Surely it's not safe for the baby." I shake my head with the words, unable to keep the panic out of my voice.

Theo grabs two beers out of the fridge on his way past and offers one to me over the counter. "I'm sure Misty will keep that in mind as she makes one of those bracelets of hers. Anyway, she's your mate. Pack magic may even negate Misty's wards."

My eyes widen as I place the bottle on the side before I squeeze it too hard in my tightening fist. "I wasn't thinking about the wards. It was the customers I was more concerned about." I pull my phone out of my pocket and before even unlocking the screen, I place it back in my pocket. "I need to buy her a phone," I mutter to myself. "You need to call Bel and tell her not to take Selena to the bar. I thought they'd be going to Misty's apartment, not the bar."

Theo pulls out his phone, glancing at the locked screen but doesn't bother to put his pin in. Maybe he has one of those thumbprint things set up. "It's only lunch. They'll go to Misty's apartment for a couple of hours first." He places his phone back in his pocket and grabs my beer off the side before marching towards his office. "If we get through business quickly, you can get to her before they even leave Misty's apartment."

I grunt, not entirely happy with his decision. But not having any of the Pack's contacts in my phone, it's not like I can do anything else about the situation.

16

WE BELONG

I give the bracelet a nervous glance as Bel ties it around my left wrist. It looks like an ordinary leather bracelet, but it's supposed to counteract the magical wards on Misty's bar, the ones meant to repel humans. "Are you sure this is going to work?"

Bel runs her hand over it. "I know it looks like any other bracelet to you, but I can sense the magic." She closes her eyes, and it looks as if she's really feeling something out of the ordinary.

I glance across to Misty as she walks in the room with her work uniform on. "The baby will be safe?" I ask cautiously. I've always wanted to go to Misty's, but I won't put my baby's life at risk. I've heard how powerful the wards are, how a human could have a heart attack if they were somehow forced to go in. Living around a pack of werewolves who think you're a ditz, means they sometimes forget what they say in front of you.

After I lost my father and brother, I wasn't the carefree girl I'd been before, but Theo helped me slowly find her again. The day Cain told me about their secret, that's when I became a nasty bitch, and played up to the ditzy image everyone seemed to be treating me as. I thought Theo would eventually tell me himself, but with every day he didn't, I completely lost myself.

A hand rubs against my bump, pulling me back to the

present to find Misty giving me a serene smile. "I wouldn't put ya baby in danger. I adjusted the spell to cover ya both. It's much stronger than the one I gave Ruby when she was a human."

"When she *was* a human?" I ask, my eyes widening in surprise.

They both snap their eyes towards me. "You don't know?" Bel asks, before shaking her head. "Of course, you don't know. We thought you were in the dark when all that happened."

"Is it something to do with her being mated to Eddie? I've put two and two together and worked that much out."

Misty looks at her watch. "I've gotta get to work. We can fill ya in on the way." She reaches out to hook onto my casted arm before thinking better of it and walking a few steps in front. "I can't believe Cain did that."

"Guilt must be eating him up." Bel glances across at me from where she's walking beside me, her arm hooked in my good arm. "His wolf will be having a hard time. We protect our mates. We don't hurt them."

I sigh. "We weren't mated at the time."

"Maybe not, but his wolf has thought of you as his mate for a long time. Technicalities like that won't make a difference."

We walk out of the apartment complex, Misty giving the guard a polite "Catch ya later" on her way past. As we slip into Misty's purple VW Beetle, I change the subject.

"What did you mean about Ruby when you said she *was* human?"

Bel turns in the passenger seat to look at me through the gap between the two front seats. "Do you remember when Cain turned up and everyone was pretty much yelling at everyone?"

I nod, of course I remember that day. That's the day I saw the man I never thought I'd lay eyes on again.

"Well, she was attacked by a vampire, and Dominic, the king of the local vampire coven turned her in order to save her life."

My heart picks up speed. Surely, I didn't hear that right. "Vampire? Did you just say vampire?"

"Yes. Just remember they've existed all the time you haven't known, and you weren't killed," Bel states, before giggling at my raised brow. "That probably isn't as comforting as it sounded in my head."

"No kidding." I shake my head. Unbelievable. I'd never imagined vampires were real. But then again, if you'd ask me all those years ago, before Cain shared his secret, I wouldn't have thought werewolves were real either. "So, Ruby's a vampire." I raise a hand to my mouth as I think of all the adjustments a change like that must take. "How is she coping with all the change?"

Misty pulls into an abandoned alley and stops beside some large bins at the back of a building. Bel jumps out the car. "She struggled at first but seems to be doing well now. She'll be here once the sun goes down. She'll be more than happy to chat to you about it," Bel states as I heave myself out of the car. "Do you need a hand?"

After a bit of effort, I straighten beside the car. "Thanks, but it looks like I've got it. Although I might need to take you up on that in the next couple of weeks."

Misty lets us in and goes about opening up. I pause before the doorway, taking stock of my body, searching for any reaction to the wards that are supposed to be here. I feel… nothing. Well, nothing unusual.

"All good?" Bel asks, giving me a curious glance.

Smiling, I step over the threshold and release a breath as again, nothing happens.

"Fabulous," Bel says, before getting me seated on a stool at the side of the bar. It has no back support so I know I'm not going to last long on it, but before I can say anything, Bel tells me we'll move to a table once it starts getting busy.

An hour passes and customers have been slowly filing in. My back is aching on the stool, and I'm desperate to move but Bel is distracted, chatting to someone at the other side of the bar and I feel that if I try to slide off the stool, I'm likely to fall off the damn thing.

Warm hands glide around my back and rest on hips, causing me to jump. The stool wobbles on the spot, but the strong hands hold me steady.

"Hey, I didn't mean to startle you." Cain's breath falls over my neck in a caress, causing goosebumps to rise.

I lean into him, and my back screams out at the movement. I let out a grunt of pain as I try to reach around to rub my lower back.

Cain pushes my hands away and takes over. "I can take you home if you want?"

"No, I want to hang around for a while and see what you guys have been getting up to all these years." I let out a moan of pleasure as his hands ease away my aches.

He leans in, and I can feel a familiar hardness pressed to my back. "If you keep making noises like that, we'll have to make use of Misty's office." He presses a kiss to my shoulder before I hear him breathing in my scent. "Let's get you sat somewhere more comfortable."

"I don't think I'll ever get used to you doing that." I let him help me off the stool and lead me towards a round table near the dance floor.

He pulls out a chair and I take a seat. "And what might that be?" he asks, sitting beside me. I let out a squeal as he tugs my chair closer to him. Once next to him, he runs a finger over my shoulder and inhales in again.

"That. Sniffing me." I laugh. "It's weird."

"I can't help it. It's a were thing. You'll just have to get used to it."

Theo takes a seat opposite us and glares over at the bar. "It's her night off, yet she'll spend most of it behind the bar."

I glance over at the bar for a second and watch Bel serve a customer before I give Theo a sympathetic smile. "She did say once Lucy turns up for her shift, she'll join us. If you sit at the bar, she'll probably talk to you between customers."

He stares me down with a raised brow. "Are you trying to get rid of me." He drops his eyes to follow Cain's hand caressing the skin at the edge of my top, dropping dangerously close to my breast. "I know you're newly mated, but you're in a bar full of people. People who can smell arousal."

I slap Cain's hand away, earning a laugh from the pair of them. "Aw, beautiful, I can't help it. You bring the sex beast out of me."

"Oh my God." I lift my hands to cover my flaming cheeks. "Maybe I should have gone home."

"And miss out on all the fun to come? No way," Bel states as she drops into Theo's lap. He thoroughly ravishes her mouth, making me feel the need to avert my eyes.

"I thought you were waiting for Lucy to arrive." Theo's voice makes it clear it's safe to look back in their direction, and I do in time to catch him breathing in her scent, just like Cain seems to love doing. I can't help but grin at the sight.

"You were staring daggers at the customers. Misty said I should come over here before you scared them all away." Bel leans in and gives Theo a gentle kiss on the lips, which he instantly deepens.

"Oh, come on!" Ruby shouts from behind us. "I thought moving out meant I wouldn't have to witness you two playing tonsil tennis anymore." I glance across to Cain as Ruby kisses his cheek. I can't help but look for vampire signs, but she doesn't look any different to any other time I've seen her. She's got the same long wavy blonde hair and green eyes, which are a sage rather than emerald like Theo's. "I hear congratulations is in order." She looks at Cain with raised eyebrows, and I feel like shrinking into my seat. When it became clear that Theo was never going to tell me about his secret, I started to resent him. I never cared what the pack or the Wilson family thought of me. Now, I do. I love Cain, and I want everyone he loves to like me. I don't want them to think I'm the evil bitch I once was. I was only that person because the resentment was eating me up.

Cain slides his hand down my arm and takes my hand in his, making me wonder if he's sensing my anxiety somehow. He did say there may be some weird feelings that may come through to me, like a side effect of our mating, but I haven't felt any different. So I hadn't thought it would have affected him either. I'll have to remember to ask him later when we are alone. "Thanks, Rubes. It's been a long time in the making."

Ruby gives him smile and a nod before turning her smile on me. "Welcome to the family again, Selena. I'd love to have a chat and compare our mate bonds. The one between me and Eddie seems to be normal. Although when I'm dead for the day, it's completely severed. Like I'm really dead..." She frowns, before carrying on. "Which I am, so that makes sense... I guess."

"The first time that happened I freaked out. I shifted and tore up the bedroom." Eddie sidles up to Ruby, who spins around and throws her arms around him before planting a kiss on his lips. "Hey, baby. I missed you too," he says as he pulls away.

"Weren't you just telling me off for playing tonsil tennis?" Theo laughs. "Hypocrite," he jokes, with a shake of his head.

"There was absolutely no tongue action. I do know how to behave in public, unlike some," Ruby snaps back while peeling herself off Eddie and taking a seat next to Cain.

Eddie pulls a short stool up beside Ruby and straddles it. "I can attest to that. I'm disappointed to say there was absolutely no tongue action." He looks genuinely disappointed.

I can't help but laugh.

Cain slides into my space, my laugh having obviously caught his attention. "I think we should show them what a proper kiss looks like."

Before I can argue, his lips are on mine and I'm melting into his arms. A shrill wolf whistle has me pulling away, remembering we have an audience. "It's looking like couples' corner over here. Maybe I should take these drinks and drown my sorrows elsewhere."

Eddie stands and reaches for one of the drink-laden trays Billy's holding. "Don't even think about it, buddy."

"Ginger ale for the beautiful Selena," Billy says, giving me a wink as he places a glass on the table before me. My eyes widen in surprise as I wonder how he knows what I drink. "I've seen you drinking the stuff by the gallon at the house," he says with a shrug, correctly guessing my thoughts.

"Thanks, Billy." I give him a grateful smile. "It's one of the only things that kept my stomach settled in the beginning. Now I think I've become addicted to the stuff." I laugh.

Billy pulls a chair over from the next table and sits to my right. "*Holy shit!* What happened to your arm?" His eyes are focused on my cast.

Cain stiffens on my other side, no doubt dwelling in the guilt once again. I give him a quick glance and seeing his jaw tight with tension, I give his hand a comforting squeeze. "My ex turned up yesterday. Things got a little heated."

"*I* got a little heated," Cain snaps, pulling his hand from mine to run it through his dark hair.

I ignore the numerous gasps around the table and turn to him. "Cain," I plead. He's staring across the room and I don't want to use my cast-covered arm to turn his head so I squeeze his knee. "Look at me, Cain. Please." He turns his head stiffly.

"You didn't do it intentionally."

I let my eyes roam around everyone at the table, pinning each one of them with a glacial stare, daring them to disagree with me. "He was fuming at my ex, who tried to drag me away."

I turn back to Cain, demanding with every fibre of my body that he listens to me. "*I* put my hand in yours, even though I knew you were in a rage and on the edge of shifting. *I* did that Cain. Do you hear me?"

I hold my breath, waiting for him to reply or even show any sign of listening.

His eyes close and I slowly lean back in my seat, thinking he's come to his senses. "You sound like a domestic abuse victim, blaming yourself." His words are whispered, but at a quick glance around the table, I can see the others heard him too. And by the pitying looks on all their faces, they agree with him.

Anger surges through me. "For fuck's sake, it was *me!*" I slam my cast on the table, regretting it the second my hand starts to throb. I school my features, not wanting anyone to know about the extra pain. My drink topples over and I scoot my chair back before the liquid pours off the edge of the table and soaks into my floor length maxi dress. Cain storms off towards the bar, leaving me watching him and wishing he would just think about this rationally.

Billy places a firm had on my shoulder as I move to follow him. "He'll be back. He just needs a breather."

Cain might not be listening to reason, but I sure as hell want everyone else to take my word for it. I turn away from Cain and look at Theo. He's the leader. If he understands, everyone else will. "It wasn't like he's making it sound." Tears fill my eyes. I don't want them to think badly of him. He's hating himself enough for everyone.

"Selena. Sweetheart." The term of endearment startles me to glance in Bel's direction, hoping it didn't upset her. She gives me a reassuring smile as she traces a finger over the back of Theo's hand. "We don't blame him. Hell, if I were in his shoes, I would have probably done the same thing. You're human. You break easily."

Billy strokes my forearm comfortingly.

"But it doesn't mean he has to like what he did," Theo finishes. His eyes flick behind me and I know Cain is there.

I can feel him.

A gentle caress over my skin, like static electricity—only it's Cain. It's the first time I've felt something like this. Closing my eyes to focus better, I feel a tugging in my mind's eye and become overwhelmed with love.

I turn my head and pop open my eyes to find Cain looking down at me with the same love in his eyes. Sensing a pang of guilt, I know it's coming from Cain. Excitement pours through me as I realise we really do have a mate bond. Cain's smile grows, and I can only assume he's feeling my excitement. I let my love pour through the bond.

Cain places a glass of ginger ale on the table over my shoulder and slides into his chair before leaning into me, his hand wrapping around my neck and his fingers gripping the hair at the base of my skull as he kisses me senseless.

"*Fuck!* It's getting hot in here. What the hell did we just miss?" Billy picks up his pint of beer and drains the glass. "I need another fucking drink."

Cain doesn't take his eyes off mine as he pulls away. "Our mate bond just kicked in, didn't it, beautiful?" At a loss for words after that kiss, I nod my agreement as his hand snakes around my neck and he runs his thumb over my bottom lip.

"Did I hear ya say ya needed a drink?" Misty catches our attention, and we all seem to look towards her in unison as she places a pint in front of Billy before giving him a wink. "Hi, guys. I figured I'd come and visit you while I have my break."

"Thanks, doll, you're a mind reader," Billy says as he takes a gulp of the amber liquid.

Misty glances around, seeming to look for a spare chair. "Nope, ya just shouted loud enough for everyone to hear ya," she states before leaning a hip on the back of his chair.

Billy sticks his leg to the side a little. "Here." He pats his knee. "You can't spend your break on your feet."

Misty takes him up on the offer and I catch sight of Billy's hand slide along her back. I can't help but wonder if there may be something happening between the two of them that nobody knows about. I glance around the table and see a questioning look on Theo's face, confirming my suspicions.

"Well, if it isn't my favourite people, all at one table," a well-spoken male voice states.

Theo growls, eliciting a playful smack from Bel. "Behave."

Theo sighs. "Dominick," he greets with a slight nod. *Dominick.* The name rings a bell and it takes me a second to remember where from. Dominick is the king of vampires here in Mount Roxby. Misty and Bel were only talking about him earlier.

I lean into Cain's side a little more as I try to hide a shudder. I'm not sure I like the thought of him being a king of people who suck blood. Jesus, my sister-in-law is one of those people. I flick my eyes to Ruby before flicking them to Dominick to try and find any similarities, some sign of vampirism, but I see nothing that screams vampire. Ruby looks just as she always has and Dominick looks like a regular guy. Quite possibly a little arrogant, but there are a lot of regular guys who have that trait.

Dominick comes to a stop behind Billy, placing his hand on Billy's shoulder. Cain stiffens beside me, and I wonder if it's some supernatural creature political stand, but Dominick suddenly gives the shoulder a gentle, almost intimate, squeeze before letting go. "Ruby, I haven't seen you at the compound lately. Are you keeping well fed?"

"I haven't seen *you* at the compound lately, and considering I've been feeding there most days, that's somewhat strange." The curiosity in Ruby's voice seems to interest everyone around the table. Theo sits forward slightly in his seat, and Bel squints at Dominick as if she's trying to read his mind. Although she's more likely to be trying to sense his emotions, since she's an empath. That was something else she managed to fill me in on today. I actually learnt a world of information in just those few hours I spent with her and Misty.

"I guess I've been otherwise engaged." Dominick glances across at Bel and frowns, no doubt at her scrutiny.

"You're seeing someone. You actually care about them," Bel states, sounding shocked at her discovery.

Dominick waves a hand dismissively. "I do have the ability to care for another person. I'm not a complete monster." He shakes his head. "Anyway, I do believe you wanted to ask me something, Theo?"

Theo clears his throat before speaking. "Yes. Have you given permission to a fox or a skulk of them to enter my territory?"

"*Our* territory," Dominick corrects. "No, the lion was the last shifter I allowed in, and I believe after that, we agreed you would deal with shifter request from then onwards."

"We did, but we had a fox turn up at the pack house, and I wanted to make sure they didn't have permission before I retaliated." I shiver at Theo's threat of retaliation. Stu is a dangerous man, and although I know Theo and Cain aren't weak, the thought of them fighting with him has me scared.

Cain's arm around my shoulder rubs up and down my bicep. "Hey, everyone will be fine. It's what we do," he says, clearly catching onto to my feelings through the bond and putting two and two together.

Misty jumps off Billy's knee. "Well, it's been entertaining, but my break's up. I'll try and catch ya'll later."

"I'll walk you back to the bar," Dominick says, offering Misty the crook of his arm, but not before running a finger over the back of Billy's neck. Glancing around the table, I don't see anyone else react to the discreet move.

Misty takes his arm and hugs it to her body. "Well, thank you, kind sir."

"Misty! We have a lot to talk about, girl," Bel calls across the table as Misty and Dominick walk away. It seems she's come to some conclusion I haven't.

"Sure thing," Misty shouts.

Eddie turns to Bel after watching Misty and Dominick walk away. "What do you know that we don't?"

Bel tucks a strand of her hair behind her ear and flicks her eyes away from Misty, letting them fall on Eddie, but not before they drift over Billy a second too long. "I'm sure we'll all find out soon enough. When it's set in stone."

I lay my head against Cain's shoulder and close my eyes as I listen to the chatter around the table. I haven't felt like part of a family for a long time. It's so nice to finally feel like I belong. I place my hand over my bump as the baby kicks and I correct my thought.

We belong.

17.

SURPRISES SUCK

CAIN

As the weeks pass, I realise I need to get out of the pack house. Having people around constantly is too much for someone who's been a lone wolf for such a long time. Plus I want some privacy with my mate—which is nigh-on impossible in such a busy house. With this in mind, I've made arrangements to take Selena to view an apartment in town. I'm hoping she'll like it.

"Okay. Let's escape before I get another foot to the bladder. This baby seems to be enjoying making me suffer today." Selena comes into view and I push off from the wall I was leaning on. "What's this surprise you have anyway?"

Sliding my arm around her, I lead her out the door. "You'll find out when we get there."

Selena buckles herself in the passenger seat with a huff. "Surprises suck. Every time."

I lean over the centre console and place a kiss on the tip of her nose. "Not mine. Everyone loves my surprises."

She pins me with a serious look. "Don't say I didn't warn you."

The lift doors close and I push the number eight, making the lift start its incline. Turning to face Selena, I catch sight of her wince. "Are you okay?"

Selena takes a few shallow breaths. "Yeah. The beast was pushing on a nerve. It's all good now." She gives me a reassuring smile.

The lift suddenly jerks to a stop, and I reach out to steady Selena as she jolts forward. *"Fuck!"*

"Cain, tell me this lift is going to go again." Her eyes, wide with panic, lock on mine. "I don't want to be stuck in here."

I push the Emergency Call button before pulling her into my arms. "Someone will answer our call, and they'll have it up and running in no time, beautiful." She stiffens in my arms as her tension doubles the longer we listen to the ringing through the speaker. The speaker falls silent and I push the button once again.

After another round of unanswered ringing, I pry my phone out of my pocket and dial the estate agent. "Hi, David. It's Cain. You showed me round number sixteen in Sanori House."

"Yes, did your wife like it?" he asks, his voice high in excitement at the prospect.

I flick a glance to Selena as she steps out of my hold and paces the confines of the lift. "She hasn't had a chance to see it yet. We're currently stuck in the lift, and no one is answering the emergency call. I was hoping you'd know who to call?"

"I'll get on with the building manager and make sure someone gets to you ASAP." His voice is sharp and to the point, which makes me feel comforted in the fact that he'll do all he can to get someone to us. He wants a sale after all.

"Tha—"

"Cain!" Selena's panicked voice cuts me off.

I drop the phone from my ear and focus my attention on

Selena, who's looking at me through wide eyes on a dangerously pale face.

"I think my water just broke." Her words send a wave of terror through me.

I shake my head. "Maybe it was a bladder kick and you didn't realise."

"I haven't fucking pissed myself, Cain," she snaps angrily, her hands fisting at her sides.

My eyes drop the puddle beneath her feet. "Shit. Shit. Shit," I chant. Pushing the Emergency Call button once again.

Selena grabs hold of the handrail on the wall, her cast making a clanging noise as it hits the metal. She bends at the waist, all the while groaning. "Please let this be Braxton Hicks," she pleads. The terror in her voice makes my heart sink. *Focus, dammit! She needs me.*

Remembering my phone, I call the only person I know who's been through childbirth.

"Hello." Mum answers on the second ring and I relax marginally at the sound of her voice.

"Mum, Selena's in labour." A million questions run through my mind, but I ask the most important one. "What do I do?"

"She's not due for another couple of weeks. You need to get her to the hospital to be safe."

I rub a hand over Selena's stiff back as she lets out another groan. "I would, Mum, but we're currently stuck in a fucking lift." I take a deep breath and realise Selena should be doing the same. "Breathe, Selena. Do you recall what you learnt in those birthing classes?"

"I took her to most of them. Put me on speaker," Mum demands, and I place the phone on the floor. "Selena, remember how they taught you to pant?" The sound of Mum panting comes through the phone and Selena joins in.

"That's it, beautiful. You're doing great."

"Cain, you need to keep her calm and breathing, just like

she is. I'm going to hang up now so you can call an ambulance. Tell them what's happening and they'll get a midwife on the line. Okay?"

"Okay," I reply to the silent phone as the line goes dead.

Selena whimpers into the empty lift. "I can't have this baby in a lift."

I turn her so she's facing me, ducking slightly to catch her eyes with mine. "You can do this, Selena. I know you c—" My sentence is cut short as she leans into me, gripping my shoulders with fingers that feel like talons and letting out a pain-filled cry.

I rub circles on her back until her hold loosens and I assume whatever caused the pain has passed. Picking up my phone off the floor I quickly dial 000. The call is connected immediately.

"This is emergency services, what service do you require?"

"Ambulance… and fire brigade," I add, thinking about our predicament. "We're stuck in a lift."

"What is the address and location of the lift?"

I reel off the address hoping the estate agent already has someone working on getting us out. Selena lets out another pain-filled cry that tears my attention from the phone. I place it onto the floor after ensuring its once again on speakerphone.

"Can you tell me who's injured, sir?" asks the female on the other side of the call.

"My wife's in labour." Remembering the midwife Mum mentioned, I bring it up. "She needs a midwife."

"Okay, sir. I have a midwife coming on the line. While we wait, let me get your names and a few details about your wife's pregnancy."

"Cain and Selena. She's—"

"Thirty-eight weeks," Selena says through gritted teeth.

"I'm just going to relay your information to the midwife and then she'll take over the call."

Selena slides down to the floor and reaches out for my hand with her cast-covered one. "I'm scared, Cain. What if something goes wrong?"

I sit down beside her and brush some loose hair from her sweat-coated brow. "I won't let it."

"This isn't an enemy you can just cut down," she snaps. Her fear is thick in the air causing my wolf to stir. He wants to protect her, but there's nothing he can protect her from. I tell him as much as I push him back down.

"Hello, Cain. Are you still there?" A new voice speaks over the phone.

"Yes." I jump forward, ready to do anything the midwife directs me to.

"Selena, I hear your baby has decided to surprise you with an early appearance." Her voice has a calming quality to it, which I guess is good for situations like this. "My name is Katie, and I'm going to talk you through this until the paramedics arrive."

I take a deep breath to centre myself, knowing I need to stay as calm as possible for Selena's sake.

"Cain, the first thing I need you to do is take a look and see how things are coming along."

I steal myself. Mentally preparing myself for what I may see. I've seen the videos of men fainting during childbirth, and I know I can't do that. I'm all she's got right now. I reach for her skirt as she lets out another cry.

"She shouldn't be in this much pain." I wish I could take her place. I reach through our bond hoping to pull some of the pain from her, having heard it's something mated couples can do. Unfortunately, nothing happens. Our bond is probably too new or maybe Selena's humanity gives it limitations.

"Cain." The voice pulls me out of my head. "Women have babies every day. You're both doing great."

Selena quietens down once again, so I decide now is the

best time to take a quick look. "Beautiful, you're doing amazing." I rub her knee comfortingly. "I'm going to take a quick look. Okay?"

"Hurry up, Cain. I think I need to push."

"Don't push just yet, Selena. Cain needs to make sure everything is okay with baby first." Katie says, her voice sounding higher pitched than it had been a moment ago. The sound makes my wolf stir, once again.

Lifting the hem of Selena's skirt, I fold it up and over her bump. I rip the edges of her underwear and part Selena's legs to get a clear view. "Holy shit, I can see the head." I shake my head at the sight. "It's too fucking big. It'll get stuck."

"*Shut up!*" Selena yells.

"Women's bodies are made for this. It'll fit just fine," Katie insists. "Can you just see the head or is it protruding?"

I give Selena's knee another squeeze. "Protruding. Is that what we want?"

"Yes. Selena, when the next contraction comes, I want you to push. Okay?"

Selena nods. "Yes."

"Isn't this all too quick? I thought labour lasted hours." My concerns are out of my mouth before I even have time to think about asking them.

"Every woman is different, Cain. Some could have been in labour for hours and not even realise it. They could just put the pain down to indigestion," Katie says calmly.

Selena licks her lips and looks at me guiltily. "I've been having cramps all morning. I thought it was just be Braxton Hicks. It's too early to be in labour. I was told most first-time mums have to be induced."

Taking a deep breath, I turn my focus back to the matter at hand. "Okay, Katie, what do I have to do next?"

"Cain, you need to hold your hands around the head and guide it out. As the neck comes into view, you need to make sure the cord isn't around the baby's neck. Okay? That's really important."

Selena's fear presses down on me with Katie's words. I lift myself up and place a kiss on her lips, hoping to ease her worry. She shoves me away before I can say any comforting words.

"I need to push."

I drop back on my heels and place my hands where they need to be.

Selena bares down with a feral sound. The baby's head moves out fractionally, and my hands itch to be wiped on my jeans. *What if they're too slippery to catch the baby?*

"You drop my baby and I'll kill you, Cain." Selena lets out a growl any werewolf would be proud of. "I don't care if you have fangs and claws." Her last words are barely recognisable behind the growl, but I heard them loud and clear, suddenly realising I must have spoken my worries aloud.

The little head pops out before my eyes, and I instantly slide a finger around its neck, looking for the cord. "The neck's free of a cord."

"That's good," Katie says, the relief evident in her voice. "Selena, one more big push and baby will be out."

"Ready, beautiful?" I ask.

She grits her teeth once more, determination written on her features. "Now!"

I cradle the baby's head, and the body seems to slip out once the shoulders make it through. The lift is filled with the sound of a baby's wail, and I release the breath I didn't realise I've been holding.

"That sounds like a healthy cry. I've just been told the paramedics are outside. They're going to be coming through the lift doors any second now." Katie says.

"Hey, sweetie," I coo to the baby in my arms. "Come and meet your mamma." Crawling up beside Selena, I place the baby on her chest. Not moving my hands away until I'm certain Selena has a secure grip. "We have a daughter. She's just as beautiful as her mamma."

I place a soft kiss on Selena's head.

The gaze on her tear-streaked face doesn't leave our baby's. "She's gorgeous."

The doors creak open and two guys dressed in green drop in from about waist height, the lift having evidently stopped between floors. "Hi, I'm Marcus and this is Eric. You must be Selena and Cain. Congratulations," one of the guys says, placing his bag on the floor.

I step aside giving them room to get to Selena and the baby. Picking up my phone, I pocket it before anyone steps on it.

He digs around in his bag, coming out with a couple of clips and a pair of scissors. "Dad, I've got one more job for you" He holds the scissors out towards me, and I take them warily.

Eric crouches beside Selena, reaching towards the baby. "Can I have a quick look at baby? I'll get her back to you in no time."

Selena nods and I watch her loosen her hold as he lifts the baby. Marcus places a clip on the cord near the baby's tummy and another clip a couple of inches away. "Just cut right there," he says, pointing to the space between the clips.

Taking the scissors, I make the cut, surprised at how much force it takes. It's tougher than I'd imagined. I smile feeling like I've taken the last step in making her birth official. Eric steps away, handing the baby to a fireman—who's crouching on the floor in the corridor—before lifting himself up and taking the baby away. "Where's he taking her?" I ask, torn between following him and staying with Selena.

"He's just taking her into a better light. He needs to check her colour looks good." Marcus places a blood pressure cuff on Selena's arm.

I raise my eyes to her pale face and watch as her eyes roll

back. My stomach sinks and I watch Marcus work feeling helpless.

"Fuck!" Marcus places a finger on Selena's pulse. *"Eric. I need you back here, STAT!"* he shouts.

I try to listen to the pulse he's feeling for, but I can't hear anything over my own blood rushing through my ears.

Eric joins us immediately, handing the freshly swaddled baby off to me. "Your baby is perfectly healthy." He turns his attention to Marcus and Selena, crouching down beside them. "How's mum doing?"

"Her blood pressure's low. We need to transport her immediately…" Marcus's words fade off as fear grips me.

18.

VISITORS

SELENA

*M*y eyes flicker open and roam the room until they fall on Cain. He's sitting beside the bed, his head thrown back against the wall and his hand resting in a plastic cot. The baby's hand is wrapped around his index finger. Seeing the man who holds my heart in his hands, with my beautiful baby has me smiling from ear to ear. I didn't think I could love anyone as much as I love the two people in front of me.

I reach out and stroke my baby's cheek. "Hi, gorgeous. It looks like you already have Daddy wrapped around your little finger."

Cain jumps in his seat, pulling his hand out of the baby's grip causing her to cry at the loss of his finger. "You're awake. I should call a nurse." He pushes a button beside the bed as his eyes roam over my face. "How are you feeling? It was touch and go for a while." He places a gentle kiss on my lips, leaving them to linger for just a moment. "You scared me to death." He brushes back my hair before cradling my face in his hands. His face is pale and the bags under his eyes tell me he's barely slept, so I know what he's saying must be true.

"I told you, surprises suck," I say, trying to lighten his mood.

He smiles and lifts the baby out of the cot. He looks comfortable with her, as if he's done it a number of times already. "This little surprise didn't suck."

"She's an anomaly," I agree. "She needs a name."

"Well, it's good to see you awake. Baby can have some mummy cuddles now," a nurse announces as she rushes into the room. She pushes a button on the machine beside me, and the cuff I hadn't noticed around my bicep tightens uncomfortably. "Perfect," she says, reading the numbers on the screen. "Let's get rid of this and you can try breastfeeding." She pulls the cuff off my arm and undoes the tie on the gown around my neck.

Cain places the baby in my arms, carefully wedging her in against my cast. I look at the nurse dumbfound. "I don't know how to do this."

"It's instinct. Just place her little mouth near your nipple and she'll do the rest." She nods towards the baby. "Give it a try."

After pulling the gown down to expose my right breast, I guide the baby's mouth towards my nipple, just as the nurse suggested. Her little mouth roots around for a minute searching, and I start to think she isn't going to do it until she latches on with an uncomfortable suction. I look between Cain and the nurse, excited. "I did it."

"You did." Cain gives me a proud smile before standing and stretching. "I'm going to give Mum a call and let her know you're okay," he says, pulling out his phone.

"I'll hang around until you get back, make sure Mum's feeling well enough to keep holding baby," the nurse offers as she takes a seat at the side of the bed with all the equipment.

"Thank you. I won't be long." Cain leans down and places a kiss on my head and then the baby's before leaving the room.

The door has barely closed behind Cain when there's a knock on the door and Bel's head pops in the opening. "Hey, a little bird told me you were awake."

I turn my body slightly, hoping to hide my breast from Bel's view.

She strolls in as though she hasn't even noticed I have my boobs out.

The nurse glances between the two of us before standing. "Maybe we should give Selena some privacy while she feeds the baby." She tries to tuck and arm around Bel to guide her out the room.

Bel easily dodges her. "Privacy? We're like sisters. There are no secrets between the two of us." She lets out a short chuckle. I can't help but grin at Bel's words. Secrets are one thing that aren't between us any longer. I wish she really did feel like we were sisters. Unfortunately, I'm pretty sure she'll never be able to feel like that, not with the history I have with Theo. "If you have other patients you need to attend to, feel free to go. We'll be sure to ring the button if we need anything."

The nurse hesitates at the door, and I give the her a reassuring smile as she weighs me up. "Make sure you do that," she orders as she strides off.

"I wasn't expecting any visitors," I say, closing my mouth quickly, trying to get over the shock of her being here.

Bel makes herself comfortable in the seat by all the machines. "You're pack. Of course we're here. We arrived a little while ago. The nurses wouldn't let us in until you woke up."

The baby's suckling suddenly stops and I glance down to find her asleep. I lift her up and gently pat her back as she rests against my shoulder.

"We?" I ask, as Bel's words suddenly register.

"Theo, Trudy, Billy, and Misty. Cain's talking to them now. He was trying to get them to go home before I snuck in. He didn't think you'd want the fuss."

I glance at the door wondering whether I do actually want the fuss. I've not had any real friends for such a long time. My heart swells at the thought of these people wanting to visit me.

"I think I'd like a fuss." My cheeks burn in embarrassment at the admission.

The door opens and Bel stands, reaching over the bed for the baby. "I'll take the baby while you fix up your gown."

Remembering I have my boobs on show, I willingly let my daughter go, and pull up the gown. I feel Cain's energy enter the room and look up to find him holding up a bag. "They brought your bag. Do you want to freshen up before I let them in?"

"Yes, please." I glance at the baby in Bel's arms as she coos at her and knowing she'll be safe, I slide my legs out the bed and place them gingerly on the floor. I wobble slightly and lurch for Cain's arm to steady myself as he dumps the bag on the bed and reaches out to me.

"I've got you." He tucks me under his arm and slowly walks me to the bathroom. Lowering me down into the plastic chair placed under the shower, he orders, "Don't move. I'm just going to get your bag. I'll be right back." He dashes back towards the bed.

He's back within seconds. After hanging my clean clothes on the back of the door, he places a towel on the rail. "Do you want me to help or should I just stand by?"

I stand and feeling steady enough, I start to strip out of my hospital gown. I'd feel embarrassed under his scrutiny if I'd thought it was sexual, especially since I feel like a complete mess, but the tension in his shoulders tells me it's worry that's making him watch me so closely. "I'm good, I think. Just stay close, in case."

The tension in his shoulders eases with my words, and a smile spreads across his face. "I'm not going anywhere, beautiful." His words send my heart soaring as I feel more loved than ever.

I turn on the shower and step under the spray. The thought of our baby in the other room and people waiting to see us has me making quick work of it. I turn off the taps and Cain steps up behind me, wrapping me in a fluffy towel that smells of our washing powder. "Is this from home?"

"Yeah, I put it in your bag a few days ago. I didn't think hospital towels would be soft enough for you, not when you probably feel like you've just been put through the wringer." How did I manage to get myself such a thoughtful mate? I must be luckiest woman alive.

Turning in his arms, I give him a quick kiss. "Thank you for thinking of me."

"Always." He places a kiss on my forehead before stepping away and handing me my clothes, one by one as I pull them on.

I run a brush through my hair and quickly plait it to keep it out of my way before opening the bathroom door and entering the room once again.

Bel looks up from cooing at the baby and nods towards the door. "You better tell them they can come in. Theo's impatience is suffocating me through the closed door."

Feeling a little weak and hoping Bel can't pick it up with her empathic abilities, especially not while she's being bombarded with Theo's impatience, I sit on the bed and keep my smile plastered on my face. "Go put him out of his misery, Cain."

Cain gives me a long stare before striding towards the door. He pauses with his grip on the handle. "You need to remember we have a bond. I'll tell them it'll have to be a quick visit." Not giving me a chance to argue, he opens the door and tells them exactly that.

Theo playfully slaps him in the chest as he passes. "Stop being so overprotective." Theo walks up to me and places a kiss on the top of my head. "Congratulations, Lena. Now let me have a look at our precious new pack member." He makes quick work of crossing the room and taking the baby out of his mate's arms.

"How are you doing, sweetie?" Trudy's question catches my

attention, and I flick my eyes towards her. "You look shattered. We won't stay long." She rubs my hand with hers and calls over to Theo. "Stop being a hog, Theo. I want to hold my grandbaby."

Her words make my heart flutter. Part of me can't believe that this wonderful family is accepting my baby as if she is their own blood. Seeing Cain hovering over Theo ready to jump in the second he can, makes me certain Cain will be the best father this baby could ever wish for. My heart is full to bursting with the amount of love I feel for Cain.

Trudy carefully slips her hands under the baby and Theo releases his hold. All the while Cain's hands hover underneath the transfer; clearly he's concerned that the baby may fall.

"Support the head," he orders.

Trudy gives him a glare as she steps out of his reach. "I have held a baby before, Cain." She rolls her eyes before turning her attention on me. "Does this little beauty have a name yet?"

I glance at Cain. We haven't exactly had a chance to talk about a name yet. After doing all the silly things I could try, to predict the baby's sex I'd been certain I was expecting a boy so I only had boy's names picked out. "Do you have any favourites?"

A small smile crosses his face and he lifts a hand to his chest. "Me? You want me to name her?"

"I can't think of anyone better than her daddy to give her, her name," I say, hoping he can feel my honesty through our mating bond.

He makes it across the room in two strides. His hand sliding around my neck in a possessive gesture as he crushes his lips on mine. "I fucking love you," he says, pulling back and resting his forehead against mine. "I love Olivia too. With my whole damn heart."

"Olivia?" I lean back and raise a brow in question.

"Olivia. Our daughter." Releasing me, he steps over to Trudy and takes our little girl out of her arms, settling her small body against his broad chest. "She's beautiful. She needed a beautiful name too."

I smile as he brings her towards me. "Olivia." I test the name on my lips and as I watch her in his arms, I decide the name fits her perfectly. "It's perfect."

Trudy leans over Cain's shoulder and strokes Olivia's hair. "The question is does my grandbaby like her name?"

Olivia releases a loud tommy gun-sounding fart, causing us all to laugh.

Theo looks at Cain and doubles over. After a few moments, he catches his breath enough to get a few words out. "On that note, we'll leave you to it." He waves a goodbye as he places his arm over Bel's shoulder and leads her towards the door, wrapping his spare arm around Trudy as he passes her.

"Maybe I should stay, at last to help change the nappy. I'm pretty sure that's more than air." She tries to fight against Theo but has no luck whatsoever as he tugs her out the room.

"I'll be fine, Mum. It's not the first dirty diaper I've changed, and it certainly won't be the last," he says, digging one-handed through the bag on the end of the bed. He changes the diaper like a pro, making it clear to me that he actually has done it before. Many times.

After popping the last stud on the baby grow, he lifts our complaining baby and holds her out to me. "I think this little princess wants her mummy."

I happily take her, glad to have her back in my arms. "Hey, Olivia, are you a little hungry again?" I ask as she searches with her mouth when I pull her against me. I glance up at Cain. "What do you think? She did fall asleep when I was feeding earlier."

"That looks like a hungry baby to me." He gives me a warm smile as he sits on the seat beside the bed. I'll have to ask him about his baby experience when I'm not concentrating so hard on feeding Olivia properly.

19

HOPE AT LAST

CAIN

I glance back at the baby seat in the rear-view mirror for the fifth time since driving away from the hospital.

Selena lets out an amused giggle. "We haven't even left the car park yet. Seriously, Cain, you need to calm down." She glances at the seat over her shoulder. "She's sound asleep and perfectly fine."

I sigh. Knowing she's right, I focus my attention onto the road before me. I just want to get us home in one piece. Because of Selena's recovery from her postpartum haemorrhage, and Olivia having some weight loss, they've been in the hospital for ten days. It's been the longest ten days of my life. Having caught Olivia's biological father's scent at the hospital once or twice, I want to get them away from here and to the safety of our new home. I've been spending all the time I wasn't at the hospital decorating. The best thing is, Selena knows nothing about it. I fucking hope this secret doesn't turn out to suck.

Out the corner of my eye, I catch sight of Selena straightening in her seat as I pass the turnoff to the pack house. "Where are we going?"

"We're going home," I announce.

"You just missed the turnoff." She laughs. "Are you still focusing on the baby?"

I let part of the secret drop. "I said we're going home. Not to the pack house."

She turns her head sharply to look at me. "What?" The word comes out loud, and she grimaces, flicking her eyes to the baby to check she didn't wake at the sound. Selena's shoulders relax, clearly satisfied at what she can see.

She lowers her voice. "Have we got somewhere of our own?"

I smile at her before focusing back on the road, making sure to take the correct turn.

I pull to a stop outside of a family home that will be perfect for us, even as we grow as a family. I didn't like the idea of Selena and Olivia getting stuck in a lift, so an apartment was out of the question. "Home sweet home," I announce as I slide out the car.

Stepping out of the car, Selena looks at the house with wide eyes. The amazement on her face makes all my work this last week worth it. "Is this really our home?"

I nod. "I signed the papers the day after Olivia was born. It's all ours." After Theo heard about our disaster in the apartment, he offered to sell me one of the pack's safe houses. Once I saw it, I knew it was the perfect home for our little family.

Selena carefully rounds the car and wraps her arms around my middle. "I love you, Cain Wilson. We are the luckiest girls alive."

Leaving my car door open, I lift her into my arms and dash to the front door, fumbling with the key as I unlock it. "I love you too," I say, carrying Selena over the threshold and then placing her gently on her feet in the entranceway before heading back to the car to collect our daughter.

Once we settle Olivia in her Moses basket, I finally get some alone time with my beautiful mate. I slide my arm over her shoulder as she cuddles into my side on the plush sofa. "Do you really like the house?" I ask, conscious of the fact that I chose all the paint and furnishings. "If you don't like how I decorated, you can change it. Just tell me what you want and I'll do it."

Selena runs her fingers over the back of my hand. "Cain, I love it. There's nothing that I would change." She lifts her head and our eyes meet. Tears well in hers. "You even had a canvas of my father and Maxie made. No one else would have thought of doing that."

I wipe away an escaped tear, and she turns her face to place a kiss on my palm. "Thank you."

"I love you, sweetheart. I'll do everything I can to make you happy." I place a gentle kiss on the top of her head before listening to the car I can hear pulling up on our drive. "I think we have visitors."

Selena lets out a small sigh before she shifts in her seat, making to move away. I tighten my arm around her. "Where do you think you're going?"

"To get our guests some drinks," she admits, still trying to wriggle out from out of my hold.

I jump out of my seat and head for the kitchen myself. "No chance. You've just had a baby. I think you deserve to be waited on."

Footsteps approach the door and feeling the pack energy coming from them, I quickly invite them in without raising my voice, knowing they'll hear me and saving them from waking Olivia up with a knock on the door. I go about making some tea and coffee while listening to Theo greeting Selena. His footsteps then get louder as they head in my direction.

"You did a great job of decorating this place."

I turn to see his eyes roaming around the room as he leans back against the counter opposite me.

"Does Bel want tea or coffee?" I ask, feeling a little bad not knowing what my alpha's female drinks.

"She's a coffee girl." Theo rubs at the back of his neck.

I tilt my head, listening to the voices coming from the other room. "Who else is here? I can hear Eddie and…"

"Chloe and Mum. Ruby will be arriving as soon as the sun goes down." He gives me a guilty look as I pull more cups out of the cupboard. "I did try to talk them out of visiting, but once they heard I was coming, they all had to jump in the car."

I pour the drinks, coffee for everyone, except Selena. I take what I can carry, making sure to pick up Selena's tea, before nodding at the rest sat on the side. "You might as well make yourself useful and hand those out. They're all the same."

After giving everyone their drinks, I sit down on the arm of the sofa next to Selena, since Mum seems to have stolen the seat I'd vacated. Olivia's bellowing cry comes loud and clear through the baby monitor on the coffee table.

Selena eases up from her seat. "She'll need feeding." She glances around the room. "I won't be long," she announces.

She takes a few steps towards the hall before turning her eyes on me. "Any chance you could come help set things up?" She solemnly raises her cast-covered arm in answer to the question that she must have seen in my eyes. She can't lift the baby out of the cot with the cast, not safely anyway. She had an X-ray whilst in hospital, which unfortunately showed it wasn't healed enough to be removed. I have a feeling Selena will be ringing Zainab in the next couple of days and begging to have it cut off regardless of the consequences. I see the frustration in her eyes every time she can't do these things on her own.

I stand and stride towards her. "Anything you need, beautiful."

Taking my hand in hers, she gives me a small smile.

It only takes a couple of minutes to settle the two of them in on the rocking chair in the corner of the bedroom. "Give me a shout when you're ready to come back through to the lounge." I place a kiss on Olivia's head and then one on Selena's before heading back to our guests.

They're all talking between themselves as I walk back in the room. The mention of foxes catches my attention and I focus on what Theo is saying to Eddie as I sit in Selena's empty space.

"…foxes in town?"

Eddie shakes his head. "No, Ruby said Dominick and his vampires haven't seen any evidence of a skulk of foxes living in town. Which makes sense since neither have we. I'm thinking they must be just outside the territory to be able to come and go with so much ease."

Theo looks to me. "Are you sure it was his scent at the hospital?"

I nod. "Without a doubt." I wouldn't ever forget his scent. "I've been checking around here every time I come home from the hospital, but I haven't caught it. I'm hoping he doesn't know we aren't at the pack house."

"You might be right. He's definitely been snooping around the pack house. I picked up the scent from the hospital in the surrounding bush this morning," Eddie admits, before adding more. "He's getting around in a car though because it just disappears at the roadside."

"I'm going to put a couple of wolves on patrol tonight. Hopefully we can catch him snooping and interrogate him," Theo says before draining his cup.

Bel stands, taking Theo's empty cup and grabbing Eddie's too. She walks off into the kitchen, Mum and Chloe following closely behind.

A gentle knock sounds on the front door before it instantly opens and Ruby walks in. I glance behind her and notice it's dark and we're all sitting in just the light of the TV. Realising Selena must be in the dark, I give Ruby a brief hug and head back into the bedroom.

"Hey! Are you okay?"

"I think we're done. I was just about to give you a shout." I can hear the smile in her voice, and as I get close to her, I can even see it with my wolf's eyes. I scoop Olivia out of her arms while Selena straightens her clothes.

With Olivia tucked safely in my right arm, I offer Selena my other hand and pull her out the rocker. As we step into the brightness of the lounge, I squint against the light. Flicking my eyes towards Olivia, I watch her little baby blues squinting too.

"Hey, princess. That nasty light is bright, isn't it?"

Mum jumps up off the sofa. "I didn't think. Should I put the lamp on instead?" She steps towards the light switch.

"It's fine, Mum. She's getting used to it now." I turn my attention back to Olivia whose wide eyes are looking up at me, seemingly enraptured.

"He enthrals me too, baby," Selena says, looking at Olivia over my bicep.

Ruby pulls Selena into her arms. "Congratulations." Quickly releasing Selena, she looks over my arm at Olivia. "She's so beautiful."

"Do you want a cuddle?" I offer Olivia across to Ruby.

Ruby gulps and flicks her eyes from me to Olivia. They finally fall on Selena. "You trust me?" The astonishment in her voice causes my heart to hurt.

"Of course," Selena says, her voice full of certainty. She gives Ruby a gentle squeeze on her upper arm as she passes her, heading back towards the sofa.

Ruby reaches out and gingerly takes Olivia out of my arms, settling her against her own chest as she walks towards Eddie, who stands, offering her his armchair. Once she's seated, he rests on the arm of the chair, leaning over her and talking nonsense to Olivia. *They'll never have that with their own children.*

My heart lurches in my chest at the thought, taking my breath away for a split second. Selena reaches out and takes my hand as I sit on the arm beside her, giving it a comforting squeeze, probably having caught on to my thought through the mating bond. Taking my eyes off Ruby and Eddie, I catch the warm smile she gives me as we lock eyes. "It's back," she says in confirmation.

Leaning in, I give her a quick kiss on the top of the head. "I love you."

"Oh, I was meant to tell you…" Ruby lifts her gaze from Olivia and locks them on Theo's. "Dominick's sending Casanova out to hunt for the fox tonight."

His eyes widen in surprise. "I didn't think he wanted to dirty his hands with *mutt* business?" The word mutt drips with disdain.

Ruby smiles down at Olivia, who is gripping her finger in her little fist. "Dominick hasn't used that word in a while. I think he's warming to the pack."

Theo lets out a laugh. "Or just a certain pack member."

I glance up at him in surprise and catch Eddie's sharp turn of the head in the corner of my eye. So, I'm not the only one surprised to hear that. "He's dating a pack member?"

He grunts and focuses back on Ruby, seeming to dismiss my question. It leaves me to wonder if Ruby is the pack member Theo is talking about, since she is one of Dominick's now, too. "He's mine to interrogate, so if Casanova finds him, he brings him to me."

Ruby nods. "Dominick understands and respects that."

A growl rumbles up my chest and escapes my mouth. *"Mine!"* my wolf demands. I clear my throat whilst pushing my wolf down. "I need to be there, Theo." My words sound like a beg to my own ears, and seeing the sadness reflected in Theo's eyes, he heard the same.

Selena's hand tightens on mine. "Stu's still in town? I thought he'd left." The tremble in her voice has me kneeling in front of her.

Cupping her face in my palms, I stare into her eyes, making sure she sees I mean every word I'm about to say. "He's not coming anywhere near you. He doesn't even know we're here. Okay?"

The terror is clear on her unnaturally pale face. She nods, but not at all convincingly.

Holding her eyes with mine, I push all the love I have for her through our mate bond in the hopes of her feeling how much I'm willing to protect her. "You heard Ruby and Theo. Everyone is on high alert, even Dominick and his vampires. You and Olivia are safe."

20.

OURS

SELENA

I glance at my watch and hope Cain returns from his pack business soon. He's been gone longer than I expected and I don't want Olivia to wake up before he returns. I wouldn't be able to pick her up with this stupid cast on my arm. At least after tonight I should be able to look after my daughter alone. Cain has promised to take me to see Zainab, and I've already decided that I don't care what the X-ray shows. I want this damn cast removed.

A clanging noise catches my attention. I reach for the remote and mute the TV as I glance around the room, straining to hear the noise again. The hairs on my body stand on end and a sudden sinking feeling hits my gut. My instincts scream at me.

Something isn't right.

Another thud comes from the direction of the bedrooms. I rise from my seat and head that way. We'd only put Olivia down a short while ago, and she's not big enough to be making noises like that.

I push the door open and catch sight of someone climbing out of the broken window. My heart races and my eyes immediately fall to the cot. My stomach plummets at the sight of it empty, as the world around me seems to slow down.

"Olivia!" I scream like a banshee. *"My baby. Give me my baby."*

Climbing out the window after them, I ignore the glass cutting into my feet. Someone has my baby and I need get to her back. *"Cain!"* I scream, needing him here. I know he's got no chance of hearing me from Theo's though.

Chasing the person through the yard as fast as my legs will carry me, they get further and further ahead. Reaching the line of trees, I fall against one, gasping for breath as I frantically search the bushes, hoping to see some sign of the person who has my baby. There's nothing. They can't be human.

Helplessness overcomes me, and I fall to my knees with a wail.

As heavy hands fall on my shoulders. I don't even turn to see who my attacker is. If they're going to take me too, I won't even fight. I'd go willingly to be with my baby.

Cain's concerned eyes lock on mine as he drops to his knees, coming face-to-face with me. "Selena, baby. Shh... I'm here."

It's only with his words that I realise I'm still screaming his name. I close my mouth and swallow past the soreness of my raw throat.

"What's happened? Where's Olivia?" He looks over my shoulder at the house, and his eyes widen.

Turning, I see Theo looking out the broken bedroom window, a grim look plastered on his face.

"Someone took her." Sobs wrack my body and I try to fight them, knowing they need any information I can give them. But all I can think about is my missing baby. "I just want her back." The sobs take over and I can't do anything to fight it.

"I've picked up a scent. I'll follow it. You look after your mate. Her feet are all cut up." Theo's words flow past me, and I barely take them in.

"We're going to get her back, beautiful. I promise," he says, his words ending on a growl.

I focus on his wolf's eyes and know he'll follow through

with that promise. He loves her as much as I do. I fall into his arms as fresh tears run down my cheeks. My helplessness eases with the comfort of knowing we have a whole pack of were-wolves ready to lay down their lives to get Olivia back.

Lifting me into his arms, Cain carries me around to the front of the house. I stiffen as I spot a couple of neighbours. *What do they think happened?*

"The police are on their way, but it's okay. Mike's a pack member. He'll smooth it all over," Cain whispers in my ear, having most probably picked up on my concerns through the bond.

I reach down to the bond to feel the comfort I know will be there only to find an empty space. "Our bond?" My voice quivers and panic flows through me. *I can't handle losing that too.*

Placing me on the kitchen bench, he rubs his hands down my arms and presses a gentle kiss to my head. "It's just a little burnt out. It'll be back."

My brows crease as I frown. "How did you know I was worried about the neighbours?"

"You stiffened the second they came into view." His explanation brings a small smile to my face. I love how he pays attention to those little things. It's like he understands me on a level that no one else has.

Leaving me on the side, he fills a bowl full of warm water and adds a little disinfectant. He then reaches into the medicine cupboard and pulls out a large first aid kit.

"They'll find her?" My question hangs in the air as I wait with baited breath for his answer.

"Yes." That one word has so much certainty behind it, it's indisputable.

I take a deep, calming breath before nodding. "Let's get my feet cleaned up. I need to be walking when she gets back." The stupid cast on my arm has interfered with everyday stuff, I don't want cuts on my feet to do the same. Thoughts of the cast have me glaring at it.

Cain lets out a chuckle. "It's not going to run off if you glare at it enough. You'll just give yourself wrinkles from frowning." He presses a kiss to my forehead.

I can tell with his joking that he's trying to make me smile and ease my worry, but I can't bring myself to do it. "I love you, Cain," I tell him as I lift my feet so we can both assess the damage.

Grimacing at the sight, he picks up the tweezers. "You just keep remembering that as I pull out all this glass, because I'm afraid it might hurt a bit."

I grit my teeth against the pain as he digs around, pulling piece after piece of glass out of my feet. Just as I'm about to tell him I can't take anymore, he places the tweezers down.

"I think that was the last of it," he announces.

Throwing my head back in relief, I take a calming breath. "Thank God for that."

A knock at the door pauses my next thought, and a familiar voice calls through the house. "Hello? Anybody there?"

"In the kitchen, Mike. Come on through," Cain replies, as he dabs at my feet with a cotton bud soaked in antiseptic liquid.

"*Fuuuck!*" I curse, batting at his arm away. "You could have bloody well warned me."

He presses a kiss to my lips. "I thought you were watching me." The anxiety on his face makes me think he must be having a hard time, being the cause of my pain. "I'm going to wrap them and then you are as good as you'll get until your body starts to heal on its own."

Giving him a small smile, I brush a wayward strand of hair off his forehead. "Thank you," I say, before turning my attention to Mike, who's walked in with a phone to his ear.

"I'll let them know." He pulls the phone from his ear and

places it in his pocket before giving Cain a grim look. My stomach plummets.

Reaching out, I take Cain's hand in mine, needing it to centre me. I squeeze it tightly as I wait for Mike to speak.

"That was Theo. The scent stopped at a road just past the bushland." His eyes drop to the floor as soon as my eyes connect with his. It's almost as if he can't bear to look at me.

My eyes drift from Mike to Cain and back again. "What does that mean?" I ask, not wanting to believe what my mind is telling me.

Cain sighs, and Mike lifts his eyes, looking from Cain's to mine in quick succession. "It means they got into a vehicle. I'm going to go back to the station and access the traffic cameras and see what I can pick up."

"Wh… what if there aren't any traffic cameras on that road?" I ask, even though I don't want to hear the answer.

Mike takes a step backwards before turning towards the front door, completely ignoring my question. "I'll be back as soon as I've got something. Eddie's on his way to Theo. He's been known to track vehicles before."

Cain gives Mike's back an absent nod, his eyes glazed as he's obviously lost in his thoughts.

I glance around the room, unsure what to do for the best. I can't give him comforting words because I don't have them. My eyes roam his body, taking in the strain of his shoulders and clenched fists at his sides. I know he needs to be out there.

"Give me your phone," I demand, my hand outstretched, waiting for him to give me it.

His head snaps in my direction, confusion etched on his face.

I wiggle my fingers. "Your phone… give me it."

He frowns, but places it in my palm without question.

Quickly scrolling through his contacts and finding Bel's

number, I press Call. My brows rise in surprise as the sound of a ringing phone comes from the front of our house.

Bel's voice calls through the fly screen on the front door as the phone call gets rejected. "Hey! Are you after me, Cain?"

"No, it was me. Come on in. We're in the kitchen." I hand the phone back to Cain and he gives me a questioning look. I want nothing more than to fall apart in his arms, but I know I need to be calm just for a little while longer because he needs to leave, and he never will if I break. Seeing his eyes flicker as his wolf comes forward, I place my good hand on his shoulder. "You need to be out there. Hunting." I give him a knowing look. "I might not be a wolf and our bond may be a little burned out right now, but I can see it in your posture and your eyes. *You need to find our baby.*"

He closes his eyes and his shoulders relax before he speaks in a guttural voice. *"Ours."* His eyes open and I know it's his wolf talking to me. He strides past Bel and out the house without another word.

Fresh tears stream down my face with the bang of the fly screen closing behind him, and I can finally fall apart.

Bel jumps up beside me and wraps an arm around my shoulders. "You did the right thing, Selena. He won't come back without her." Reaching behind her, she tears off some kitchen roll and passes it to me.

I dab at my cheeks, wincing at the roughness of it. "That's what I'm worried about," I say through the tears that don't want to stop. My thoughts run wild with what he may be about to face, and it kills me that there's nothing I can do to help.

21.

FIERCE FEMALE

CAIN

*S*eeing Selena broken on the ground caused my wolf to jump to the forefront. He pushed me to let him take over. Her terror-filled scream of my name was the only thing that allowed me to hold him back. I was the one she needed in that moment, not my wolf.

The moment she told me to find "our baby" there was no holding him back. I managed to get out the door and under the cover of the vast bush behind our property before he burst free from my skin.

He doesn't give me the chance to shake away the last tingles of pain before racing through the bushland, following the now familiar scent of the fox. As the scent dies off by the road, I skid to halt and lower my snout, trying to find it again.

Picking up Theo and Eddie's scent, I turn to see Eddie approach in his wolf form. He drops his snout in submission, releasing a small whine. My wolf recognises the compassion.

"Eddie, see what you can pick up." Theo's voice pulls my attention from Eddie. Theo is stepping out of his clothes, folding them and placing them under some thick shrub just off the road. "Time is precious. We need to catch up with that fucking vehicle." I take a deep breath and try to catch a scent that shouldn't be here. Walking in a circle, I smell diesel and rubber, making me think he must have left with a skid of tyres in his hurry.

Eddie lets out a howl and runs off down the road, having detected up on something and considering it a lead.

I hesitate, giving Theo a quick glance.

"*Go!* I'll catch up." His shift starts to take over before the last word is out of his mouth, making it sound somewhat garbled.

Chasing down the road after Eddie, Theo's energy closes in behind me. Eddie slows his pace, and I follow suit as I search our surroundings, spotting a vehicle parked at the side of the road. The hushed sound of a baby crying has my wolf wanting to race forward instantly.

"*Cain!*" Theo's commanding tone sounds in my head, stopping me on the spot.

"*Olivia,*" I say, half explanation, half beg.

Theo steps up in front of Eddie. "*We can't just rush in. We need to be smart.*" He stalks towards the van, ears perked up on high alert. Eddie and I flank him, silently following his lead.

"For fuck's sake. Stop crying." The fox's voice comes from the open side door of the transit van. I know Selena told me his name but I can't remember it right now. Steve…Sam…It was definitely an S name. "I don't have anything to feed you. You'll have to wait until Bert and Rachel arrive."

"*He's alone.*" Theo's words run through my head telling me what I'd already deduced.

Theo slinks up to the opening as Eddie and I stay back. "*Olivia's in a car seat. Let's draw him out.*"

Stalking around the other side of the van, I barge into the side of it hard enough to make it shake.

"What the fuck?" the fox cries out. His feet hit the dirt and I hear his footsteps around the van.

As he steps into view, I pounce, not giving him time to see me. He screams as I sink my teeth into his shoulder. I curse having made the mistake of missing his neck as we both hit the floor.

"He needs to be alive for us to get information from him," Theo reminds me.

I'm grateful for my silly mistake, when only moments ago I was cursing myself for it. Releasing him, I step away, poising myself and ready to take him down if he runs or starts to shift.

Theo rounds the van on two feet. "You might as well just accept defeat. You're outnumbered and your pack mates are nowhere in sight."

The fox's shoulders slump and his head drops in submission as he gets to his feet, turning his body just enough to have a view of Theo whilst keeping sight of me, too. Clever fox, not to have a wolf at his back.

Eddie steps out from behind the van in a pair of sweats, cradling a swaddled Olivia in his arms. I let out a whimper at the sight of her, and he hooks a thumb over his shoulder. "There's a pile of sweats in the back of there. It's a shifter's van after all."

Not caring to hear another word and knowing Theo has it in hand if the fox tries anything, I dash around the van and force my shift to be as quick as possible, ignoring the extra pain it brings.

Once in human form, I duck into the van and grab some sweats, pulling them on as I walk back, the hot gravel burning the soles my feet.

Eddie holds Olivia out to me as soon as he catches sight of me.

"Hello, princess. It's good to have you in my arms again." I fight back tears as I hug her against my chest. I would never have guessed I could love a baby so much.

A scuffing sound draws my eyes from Olivia, and I watch as Eddie cable-ties the fox's arms behind his back. "Found these in the van too, so thanks for that, buddy." Heavy duty cable ties

are another thing shifters tend to keep handy in their vehicle—
you never know when you'll need to restrain an enemy. The
largest and buffest cable ties you can buy are strong and won't
break even with the force of a supernatural being behind them.

Theo steps up to them and starts patting the fox down.
"Aha! Just what I'm looking for," he says as he straightens, a
phone held in his hand. After tapping the screen a couple of
times, he raises the phone to his ear and strides to the other
side of the van.

"Billy… yeah, I borrowed a phone. We're on the road that
runs parallel with Cain's, behind the bushland, and we're in
need of a lift…" He pauses obviously listening as Billy replies.
"You'll need to floor it. We've got a couple of foxes incoming
and I want to be away before they arrive."

Theo steps back around the truck wearing a borrowed pair
of grey sweats, identical to the ones Eddie and I have on and
throws the phone to Eddie. "See if there's anything useful
on there."

"So, you're the loser who kicked my ex-wife out on the
street… pregnant?" The growl behind that last word is unmiss-
able. My skin ripples as Theo's anger brushes against it.

The fox glances between me and Theo. "What… y-your…
ex—?" he stutters.

"Jesus, mate, there's no need to stutter." Theo sighs. "My ex-
wife. My brother's mate. Yes, we keep it in the family. Now
we've cleared that up… what's your name?"

"Selena didn't tell you my name?"

My laughter at the outrage on the fox's face causes Olivia to
let out a little wail.

"Shh, it's all right, princess. Daddy has you," I soothe,
watching her little eyes stare straight at me.

Theo's growl catches my attention, and I lift my eyes to see
him shoving the fox on the ground. "Don't even think about it."

"He ain't her daddy. I am," he says, venom practically dripping from his words.

Theo's fist snaps out and connects with his jaw. I smirk at the sickening crunch I hear from across the road and can't help but wonder if Theo's fist is as damaged as the fox's face seems to be? If the scream of pain the fox is letting out is anything to go by.

"Well, he can't say you didn't fucking warn him." Eddie pelts the phone through the vans open window as he heads my way. "The dude's name is Stu. That's the name he signs at the end of his texts anyway. I emailed myself the addresses in his maps history so we can check them out later."

"Good wor—" Theo stops midsentence as the sound of a vehicle approaching reaches our ears.

We all spin to look in the direction of the incoming 4x4 as it screams towards us.

I tense, ready to flee with Olivia if it's Stu's pack mates.

I catch sight of Eddie's shoulders relaxing as his eyes fall back on our prisoner. "I'd recognise that Pajero anywhere. I've been telling Billy he needs a new exhaust for months."

Grabbing the car seat out of the van, I strap Olivia in as the others bundle our prisoner into the back.

"I'll sit here." Eddie gestures to one of the folded-up seats in the rear of the car. "I can make sure Stu doesn't try anything silly."

As we drive in the opposite direction of our house, I straighten in the back seat as I lean forward to peer through the windscreen. "Where the hell are we going?"

"My place. It's the safest place for Olivia. Stu's pack—"

"It's a fucking skulk not a pack," Stu interrupts. There's a thud from the back and a grunt, which leaves me to assume Eddie kicked him or something equally as painful.

"Fine. Stu's *skulk* won't attack the pack house," Theo

announces. "Not without knowing how many of us could be there."

I stroke Olivia's little hand and she grips onto my fingers. "Selena…."

"Will be at the house when we get there. I called Bel on my way to picking you guys up," Billy says, as we turn down the private road that leads to Theo's.

I'm just lifting Olivia out of the car seat as the front door bangs open. Turning, I tense ready for impact as I see Selena running at us full pelt.

"Livie… is she okay?" Selena asks, coming to a steady stop beside me and peering at Olivia as she worries at her lip.

"She's perfectly fine. Just had a little adventure."

A commotion at the back of the 4x4 breaks out, catching Selena's attention before I get the chance to offer Olivia over.

"Is that them? The person who took her?" Evidently deciding she's correct in her assumption, she marches to the culprit.

I follow behind and spot Stu on the floor, clearly having been rolled out the back by Eddie, who is now jumping down himself and not caring about the dust cloud he kicks up in Stu's face as he lands.

"Stu?" she screeches.

Seeing her good hand fisted at her side has me quickly passing the baby off to Eddie. "Take Liv."

"You fucking son of a bitch." She gives him a swift kick in the side. Stu lets out a grunt, and she kicks him again. "*You* took my baby. You don't even fucking want her, yet you have the audacity to take her from me."

Stu lets out a pained cough. "I told you last time, my alpha wants her." He flicks his eyes to me as I step in beside Selena, ready to protect her if she needs me. "You know what it's like. If your alpha orders you to do something, you have no choice."

Selena steps closer to him, trying to block his view of me as she stares him down. "Don't expect him to be on your side. He loves her just as much as I do." My heart jumps in my chest and my back straightens as I stand proud… and somewhat turned on by my mate's ferocity.

Olivia lets out a wail and Selena turns away from Stu, heading for a flustered Eddie, who's failing to calm Olivia down.

"You're lucky my daughter's needs come first," she says, giving Stu one last filthy look.

Eddie happily hands Olivia over to Selena, ensuring she has a secure hold before stepping away. "He won't be thinking himself lucky when we've finished with him. I promise you that, Selena."

Eddie may be a couple of years younger than me, but he sure does have a good head on his shoulders. Olivia is pack and Stu has done wrong by taking her.

He's going to pay.

22.

FACE OFF

*P*ushing myself forward to follow Selena into the house, my wolf and I argue with every deliberately slow step I take. He wants to be in on the interrogation of Stu, but I know if I go in there straight away, we won't get any information out of him because he wants to tear Stu apart. *Hell, we both do.* Olivia is ours, and Stu should never have touched her.

Mum runs into the hall. "Is she okay? He didn't hurt her, did he?"

I close the door behind me as I listen to Selena trying to placate my mum. "Olivia's fine, Trudy. If she was hurt, they would've taken her straight to the hospital."

The door handle snaps off in my hand at the thought of Olivia needing to go to the hospital. Turning around, I find two-sets of stunned eyes on me.

"Are you okay?" Selena asks as she brushes her fingers over my forearm.

I open my mouth to speak, but only a growl leaves my parted lips. I clear my throat and try again. "Sorry. I didn't realise...." I shake my head, not knowing what to say. I'm not okay, and the only thing that would make me okay isn't going to help us put a stop to the danger our daughter is in.

"I get it," Selena says with a nod. "Come on. Let's go feed our baby."

Giving her a grateful smile, I allow her lead me to the lounge as I silently thank the heavens I found her. *Both of them.*

———

Twenty minutes later I'm burping Olivia over my shoulder, with Selena sipping a mint tea beside me, when Theo strides into the room through the French doors.

"I've gotta make some calls." The growl beneath Theo's words has my wolf on edge as his eyes meet mine. "Meet me in my office in five minutes." I nod my agreement as I continue to pat Olivia's back.

Bel watches Theo walk by and out of sight before jumping up off the sofa opposite us and rushing after him.

Selena's hand squeezes my knee. "Will you place her in her bassinet before you go? Trudy can help me get her out if she cries."

"Sure," I say as I stand. I gently place Olivia in the bassinet beside the sofa and wipe at the dribble of milk escaping her puckering lips with a muslin cloth. Leaning over, I press my lips to her forehead, silently promising her that I won't come back until every threat to her is gone.

A hand slides around my waist as Selena's energy wraps around me. Turning, I pull her into my arms, tucking her head under my chin.

"Thank you." The wobble in her voice squeezes at my heart.

I kiss the top of her head. "You don't need to thank me for anything," I tell her, meaning every word.

"You brought her back." She lifts a hand and wipes at her eyes, making me squeeze her a little tighter as I rub her back.

"I'm her father. I wouldn't have returned without her. She needed to be brought home… where she belongs."

The French doors slide open and Eddie walks in, a wide grin on his face. "I never thought I'd hear a fox squeal like a pig."

I give Selena one last kiss on the head before releasing my hold on her. "We best go and see what Theo has planned."

Eddie rubs his hands together in glee. "We haven't had a good pack fight in ages."

Rolling my eyes at his immaturity, I lead the way to Theo's office, pausing to rap on the closed door before entering.

"It's safe," he calls out. Bel's giggle makes me smile as we step into the room, spotting her curled up on his knee before she jumps off to stand beside his chair.

"I've had too many close calls with you two. I wasn't taking any risks," I say with a wry grin.

"Amen to that," Eddie agrees, whilst taking a seat on the sofa against the wall. "So, what's the plan, boss?"

Theo sighs and runs a hand through his short blond hair. "Stu said there were only six of them staying in the next town over." Bel strokes her fingers over his shoulders. He leans into her touch, and I watch as the tension seems to leave his shoulders. "I'm inclined to say we should take double that figure in case he's bullshitting us. We don't want to go in there too confident and have it backfire."

"I'm going." Bel's determined tone leaves no room for argument, and I look to Eddie in surprise—wondering if we should leave before things kick off between the alpha couple—and find him watching them with rapt attention.

Theo takes a deep, calming breath, seeming to steel himself before speaking. "It's too dangerous." He shakes his head.

"I'm the alpha-female, Theo. I'm going."

Theo turns his seat to face Bel, before taking her hand in his. "If you go, it'll make things more dangerous. I'll be distracted and so will most of the men. They won't like seeing their alpha-female in danger."

"If Selena was a wolf, you wouldn't stop her going—even if she was a distraction to her mate," Bel argues. "I need to go for her. I need to go for the females in our pack, those too submissive to fight. They need to know any future kids they may have will be protected and fought for by their alpha pair. Not just you, Theo. You have a mate now and that changes things." Leaning in, she gives him a gentle kiss before dropping his hand and stepping away. "I'm going to check on Selena while you guys make a plan. I'll gather the pack mates in the meeting room as they turn up, so we can all be in on the briefing."

We watch in silence as she leaves the room.

Theo takes his time turning his chair around to face us once again. "*Fuck!* She's right."

I nod in agreement. "Sadly, she is." I'm impressed with my sister-in-law. She's smart enough and strong enough to step into the role of alpha female. Bel knew exactly what the submissive wolves—who are always extremely timid and too scared to fight—would need compared to the more dominant wolves, who would jump in on their own and never need someone else to protect what's theirs.

"What's the plan, then?" Ed asks, once again sounding eager for action.

"There are five foxes at the house, one of them is the alpha. They'll have found the empty van by now and are probably making their next plan. We'll go in quietly and end it quickly. It's a built-up area, and we don't want any innocents getting hurt." Theo glances at his phone on the desk, and I give him a questioning look.

"Billy's doing a drive by on the address we got from Stu. There better not be any surprises." He rubs a hand over his face.

Seeing how stressed times like this make Theo, I'm still glad I handed the pack over to him. Despite his stress, he's handling it well. Plus he has the perfect woman for him by his side, and that thought warms my heart. "We're not going to rush in without thinking. Who'd you call in?"

"Mike, Dave, Stefan, Pete, Karl, and Trevor. Do you think I made the right call?" He raises a brow as though he's doubting his decision, which isn't like Theo.

"Add the four of us and Bel. We'll be a force to be reckoned with," I say confidently. It's not a lie. Everyone named are great fighters, and putting us together will make us a dream team. Excitement rolls through me at the thought of a fight. I can't stop wondering why the fox alpha wanted Olivia so soon. It's not like she'll show any signs of being a shifter until puberty anyway. "Who are we leaving here? We don't want to leave and have them attacking our home."

Theo grunts and nods his agreement. "I'll make that decision when Billy reports back."

Eddie glances out the window before checking his watch. "You realise Ruby is going to be gutted when she wakes up and discovers she's missed all the fun."

"It's not like we can hold off for the sun to set." I step over to the window and take in the view of the yard as I try to calm my wolf down at the thought of waiting. He's eager to get out there and fight for what is ours and, to be honest, so am I. "We need to hit them before they can arrange for more members of their skulk to arrive."

Once Billy arrived and verified Stu's confession, we came up with a solid plan and jumped into three separate cars. Trevor and Chloe were left at the pack house to protect Selena, Olivia, and Mum. Stu is still locked up and left under the supervision of another pack member. Knowing he was only following orders means he'll be released once we've dealt with his alpha. Although, the thought of him getting off scot free does grate on me. Eddie did ensure me the interrogation he received wasn't a stroll in the park.

I watch out the windscreen, memorising the route in case anything goes wrong and I need to make my way home on foot. The silence is almost deafening, and I can only assume the others in the car are doing the same. Maybe even looking for shadows that will hide our wolves if we have to flee in our wolf forms.

As our surroundings become more built up, I catch sight of Theo sitting straighter in his seat.

Billy, in the lead car, pulls over down a quiet side street and as planned, Theo drives past, parking in a vacant space on the next street along.

As we exit the car, Pete drives past in the third car, heading for the street behind the Skulk's house. Their group will be jumping over the back fence as we join Billy's group at the front of the house.

Theo throws an arm over Bel's shoulder as was walk through the street. They'd look like a regular couple on a stroll if anyone was to look out of their windows. Unfortunately, Ed and I don't look as inconspicuous.

Tension in my body builds with each step, taking us closer to our destination. A glance in Ed's direction tells me he's feeling the same from the stiffness in his shoulders.

"Guys, you need tone it down. They're going to feel you two coming and it'll blow the surprise attack," Bel states, her tone light and airy, just like her energy. I don't know how she can be so calm knowing we'll be walking into a fight. My wolf is chomping at the bit to get out and deal with our enemy.

I take a deep breath, hoping to bring my energy down a notch or two. "Sorry. My wolf's riding me hard right now."

Ed pats me on the shoulder. "I feel ya, buddy. The adrenaline is making my wolf practically impossible to calm, too."

As we get closer to Billy's car, he steps out alone—Mike and Dave having already slinked off into the street as planned.

Theo glances at his watch, causing me to look down at my own. "Everyone ready?" Bel slips out from under Theo's arm and rolls her shoulders in answer as Billy, Ed, and I all give grunts of our own agreement. He drops his arm and stares up at the house. *"Now!"*

Being the father of the kidnapped child, I lead our party up the pavement and to the front door. Without pausing, I send out a solid kick and can't hold back the smirk as the door gives under the pressure of my foot.

The sound of glass shattering throughout the building confirms the other teams are making their way in via their planned entry points.

I'm instantly met with a female, who cowers at the sight of me. The energy playing along my skin makes me wonder why the alpha would have brought such a submissive fox on this kind of a mission.

"We're here for your alpha. Point us in his direction and you won't be hurt," I inform her, trying to tamp down the growl behind my words—my wolf close to the surface. The sudden shaking throughout her body tells me I've failed.

Stepping to the side, she plasters her back against the wall, giving us access to pass by her, eyes cast down to the floor. Raising her left hand a couple of inches, she points in the direction of the back of the house.

Bypassing the lounge to my right, I follow her direction. Feeling Eddie's energy drop back behind me, I expect he's checking the lounge for skulk members.

Alpha energy presses against my skin with every step I take, confirming the female was pointing me in the right direction. Allowing my wolf closer to the surface, I push out my own energy. I may not be the alpha of my pack, but that is out of choice, not strength, or power.

I step into the kitchen and catch a fist as it slams towards my face from my left side. The fucker had tried to hide beside the door. With a twist of my wrist, I wrench him around until he's standing before me.

"Bastard!" He spits the words out angrily, spittle hitting me in the face.

Releasing his fist, I wipe my face clean with my hand. "That's not how you should be welcoming guests."

He steps back, leaving enough space between us to ensure I can't reach him without him seeing it coming.

Theo's energy presses against me, and I step aside, giving him room to enter. "I'm wondering… are we the guests or is he? He's in my territory after all."

I stroke at my chin in thought. "Huh… you have a good point there. It was still rude either way."

Our guys walk into the kitchen through the numerous entries, having round up the other foxes. The foxes gather in the middle of the room, their eyes flit to their alpha, clearly looking to him for instruction.

"You have what's mine. I have every right to be here." The determination in his voice along with the straightness of his spine tells me he's not going to back down. He's not going to leave without Olivia, and that means he won't be leaving this building alive.

"You lost any rights to claim her when you allowed Stu to kick her mother out on the street." A growl rumbles up my chest, and I fist my hands at my sides, trying not to attack before Theo gives me the okay. He's my alpha after all. How this goes down is his call.

A whistle fills the air as a knife flies right for my head. Raising my hands, I clap them together, managing to trap it between them before it hits its target. I drop it to the floor and see the blood on my palms before I feel the sting of the slices it's caused. *Fucker!*

"Fucker," Eddie calls from across the room, seemingly reading my thoughts. He starts towards the alpha, only to be held back by Billy's arm across his chest.

"No. This isn't your fight," Theo states from beside me. His words sound guttural, causing me to suddenly swallow.

I turn to Theo, needing to see his face to understand what he wants to do next. Catching sight of Bel standing behind me, leaves me feeling suddenly grateful. If I had just ducked away from the knife instead of catching it, it would've most likely found a target in her.

Theo gives me a nod, and I take that as my permission to attack. Before I can move to attack him like I'd planned, my wolf jumps forward taking control of my body. Within seconds, I'm stalking towards him on all fours. Teeth bared, a menacing growl escapes my snout.

The female I'd met in the hall earlier cowers as I pass, eyes on the floor as she plays with the hem of her shirt in her hands.

"You've made it perfectly clear you aren't leaving without his daughter so there's no chance he's going to let you leave." Theo's nonchalant comment comes from where I'd left him by the door.

The alpha fox takes a step back and looks at me with wide eyes, no doubt belatedly realising he just made a grave mistake.

My wolf snarls at the sight of his prey trying to escape.

I gnash my jaws at him, feeding on his fear that I can taste in the air. Deciding I've played with my food enough, I pounce, jaws wide to allow my teeth to sink into his neck when I make contact. As his blood fills my mouth and I rip at his neck, I start to relax for the first time since hearing Selena's earlier screams.

As the alpha fox's heartbeat diminishes, so does the threat to what's mine.

23.

SAFE AT LAST

It's been a week since Cain and the others came back from chasing the foxes out of town. It didn't slip my attention that Cain had come back wearing a completely different outfit to the one he'd left the pack house in. I didn't question him about it at the time. He came back to me in one piece and that's all that matters, regardless of what he had to do to ensure Olivia's safety. But it's been playing on my mind and I know I'll have to ask at some point. I've been to visit Alyssa a few times and even took Olivia with me once, which seemed to help bring Alyssa out of her deep sombre mood, even if it was for only a few minutes. I'm hoping it's a sign that when her baby arrives—which Cain informed me could be as soon as next week, due to werewolves having a similar duration of pregnancy as normal wolves— it'll help her heal by giving her a new focus for her life and future.

We're driving towards yet another surprise. I don't know how many sucky surprises it's going to take for him to realise they aren't worth doing.

I bite my lip as I contemplate asking about the foxes.

Cain flicks his eyes to me having taken them off the road for only a second. "Ask. I can see something's eating away at you." He blindly reaches out and gives my knee a gentle squeeze. "You might as well ask or it'll ruin the whole day."

I release a deep breath and relax into the seat at the comfort of his touch. "What happened to the foxes? Did you kill them all?"

"*What?*" His high-pitched question causes Livie to stir in her car seat. We both stare in her direction, and I silently pray she doesn't wake up until we've finished this conversation.

A second passes without her crying and Cain lets out a breath. "Do you really think we killed them all?"

Guilt runs through me for thinking such a thing, but he's spot on: I had thought that. "I didn't know what to think," I admit, feeling the need to explain more. I press on before he can react. "I know what you are and how dangerous you can be even though I haven't seen it first-hand. You came home in a different set of clothes. It was obvious your wolf had been out and I'm betting it wasn't to play."

Cain shakes his head. Seeing the unhappiness in his down-turned facial features, I grab his hand, locking my fingers in his as I feel the need to touch him. To comfort him. "I shouldn't have left you thinking like that. You've been with the pack for so long, I forget you'd been left in the dark for most of that time." Cain lets out a sigh.

I rub the back of his hand with my thumb. "Cain, it's not your fault. I should have asked sooner. Part of me didn't care... *doesn't* care what you had to do. Whatever it is, you did it to protect Olivia, and that's all that matters. I just wondered if anyone else was going to come and try to get her later... or heaven forbid take you away from me as payback for what you and Theo did to the other foxes." I swallow past the scratchy feeling in my throat, suddenly overwhelmed by the heaviness in my chest.

Cain pulls the car off the road sharply, and once the engine's switched off, he turns in his seat. "Hey, shh." He cups my cheek, lifting my gaze to meet his as he wipes a tear on my cheek with his thumb. "Nobody is coming for Olivia or me. I can promise you that. Okay?"

Seeing the truth in his sparkling blue eyes, my fear dissipates. I swallow away the lump in my throat and nod.

"Only one fox died, and that was the alpha. He wouldn't leave without Olivia, which meant I couldn't allow him to live." His piercing gaze searches my face, and for a moment, I wonder what he's looking for. A smile crosses his face, and he sits back, seemingly satisfied with whatever he sees.

"The beta fox took charge, becoming the new alpha. He gave his word that his skulk would never come back for Olivia. If I had any doubt, I wouldn't have let them leave, but they didn't even want to be there in the first place, like Stu, they were just following orders."

I slide my hand over his cheek, feeling the slight stubble under my palm. Leaning forward, I place a searing kiss on his lips, heat floods my body and I suddenly wish we were anywhere but parked up on the side of the road. I pull back before I end up climbing into his lap and taking what I need from him. "I trust your judgement. If you say we're safe, we *are* safe at last."

Tempted to lean in for another kiss, I lick my lips. Cain rubs his thumb over the wetness on my bottom lip. I can see the temptation in his eyes and the way he licks his own lips.

"Let's get back on the road, or we'll never get to our destination," he says, starting the car and pulling into a gap in the traffic as he leads us once again to our surprise destination.

*A*s Cain's pulling down a dirt track road, I get a familiar sensation, like I've been here before. Once the fields beside us start to fill with sunflowers, I know I've been here before.

"Cain," I say, my voice breaking on the one word, unable to keep the emotion hidden.

He stops at the side of the road beside the fourth field on the right. "I thought it was about time we introduced Olivia to your father and Maxie."

The thought about bringing Olivia here hadn't even crossed my mind yet, but the fact that Cain knew it's something I'd want, makes my heart almost explode with love for him. Tears well in my eyes, overwhelmed with emotions.

Cain wipes at my escaping tears. "This wasn't meant to make you sad. We don't have to get out. I can turn the car around and go home," he offers, putting his hand back on the keys still hanging in the ignition.

I place my hand on his arm. "No. I'm not sad. I'm happy. So happy that you thought of what I needed before I even knew I needed it."

Pulling the keys from the ignition, he relaxes back into the seat. "I'm your mate. It's what I'm here for."

I slide over the centre console and sit in his lap, facing him. "I love you."

He crushes his lips to mine and causing my somewhat rounder bottom—since having Olivia—to press against the steering wheel, setting off the horn. Olivia lets out a wail, and I press my forehead against Cain's as I try to contain my laughter.

He taps the side of my thigh. "Get that bubble butt out the car and I'll grab Livie."

24.

OUR FAMILY

CAIN

J let out a hearty laugh as Selena climbs out of the car, knocking the horn twice more on her way out. "Shh… it's all right, Livie. It's only Mummy and her big bubble butt," I call back to Olivia in her car seat.

Selena swats at my arm. "I swear, Cain, if you refer to my butt as a bubble butt one more time I won't be held accountable for my actions."

Holding my hands up, I give in. She shakes her head—clearly not believing my offer one iota—before walking off into the field where a few years ago we'd scattered her father and brother's ashes.

After getting out the car, I open the back and unhook Olivia from the car seat. Turning to face the field, I watch Selena, her head thrown back as she looks up to the sky, her blonde waves hanging loose as her mint green dress flutters between the flowers in the wind.

I tilt Olivia in my arms so she's looking in Selena's direction. "You see that beautiful goddess, Livie? She's your mummy. And my mate. I think that makes us both the luckiest people on the planet."

I walk through the field and come to a stop beside Selena, slipping my free arm around her waist. "Have you told them why we're here?"

She looks down from the sky, and I catch sight of the blush crossing her cheeks before she drops her eyes to her feet. "I must look like an idiot."

"Far from it, beautiful. In fact, we were just saying how you looked like a goddess. Isn't that right, Livie?" I glance at Olivia for confirmation and get a smile in return, which I take as a win. "See? She just agreed," I say, nudging Selena in the side.

Selena chuckles. "I'm pretty sure that was wind, but I'll believe you." She presses a kiss to my shoulder, and I kiss her on the top of the head before offering Olivia over to her. She takes her without question, and I slip my keys into my back pocket before taking another item out of my front pocket.

I drop to one knee at her feet.

She gasps and lifts a hand to her mouth.

Taking a deep, calming breath, I swallow the panic running through me at the thought of her possibly rejecting me. "Selena. I knew you were my mate from the first time I laid eyes on you. We've had some obstacles in our way but we finally found our way back to each other." Having seemingly forgotten how to breathe and talk, I take a quick breath. "Even though we're officially mated, for my wolf and the pack to be happy, I'd like to make things right for you and Olivia. Selena, will you marry me?" I hold out the ring I'd picked a few days ago, the one I've been dying to see on her finger.

Selena drops to her knees before me. If I wasn't so concerned about her answer, I would probably be worried about the mess her dress will be in. "Of course I'll marry you…. Oh, Cain." She presses her soft lips against mine in a quick kiss before pulling back and looking at me with wide eyes surrounded by wet lashes. "You didn't have to do this, you know? I was perfectly happy being mated, without the ceremony."

"Maybe I'm selfish, but I want to stand in front of everyone and make us a family. My family."

"*Our* family," Selena corrects me before I sink my hands in to her hair and kiss her senseless, while being careful not to crush Olivia between the two of us. I'm filled with euphoria in the perfectness of the moment. I can imagine us coming here for years to come—chasing Olivia between the sunflowers while Selena cradles another child of ours in her arms.

We may have hurdles to face in our future, but I know *together* we can get through anything that comes to try us.

The End.

EXCERPT

Please turn the page for an excerpt of

Love of Three
Mount Roxby Series, #4
A Novella.

Previously published as a short story in *Haunted by Love Anthology*.

Coming soon with extra content.

1.

NEVER UNDERESTIMATE A WITCH

Clearing the tables at the end of the night can be therapeutic—all the mess disappearing and the bar being ready for opening up the next day. Unfortunately, there are times when it isn't so good. Like tonight, when that last customer hangs around, moving with every table you clear.

I place the chairs upside down on the last table and glance around the room to make sure I haven't missed anything. All the tables leading to the dance floor are clean, and the chairs are upside down how I like them. The row of booths along the right-hand wall all have chairs upside down on the edges of the table so people know they're no longer to be used.

I turn to the bar with my cloth, preparing for my last job of the night. Well, that and nonchalantly getting the vampire who's leaning against the bar to leave.

"Look, buddy, it's time for ya to go home." I collect a handful of glasses along the bar, taking them around the other side to put them in the little dishwasher. "I wanna get home before the sun rises and I'm pretty sure you do too," I state, making it clear I know exactly what he is. I don't share his reasons for getting home before sunrise, though. I'm a witch, not a vampire.

In a flash, he's behind the bar and crowding my space.

"We could have a pretty good time between now and

sunrise." He glances around the room. "Besides, it's not like this place has any windows. We could keep going until the sun puts me to sleep."

I shudder at the thought of being stuck with his lifeless body. I take a step back, and he follows. "Look, ya need to get outta my space or I won't be held responsible for my actions."

He throws his head back and lets out a heavy laugh. These other supes always underestimate us witches. Vampires and shifters are the worst culprits. Demons seem to be the only ones who remember how dangerous we can be. "You won't be held respon—"

I cut his sentence short by throwing a spell at him with a clench of my fist. He drops his head into his hand as I squeeze his brain in my fist.

"Shiit," he groans. The pain is clearly too much for him to handle.

The front door opens and I glance that way as I step around the bar and away from the vampire.

"Is everything all right in here?" Billy, one of the local werewolves, asks from the doorway, his eyes flicking from me to the vamp.

I loosen my fist, effectively releasing my grip on the vamp's brain, but only enough for him to hear my words through the pain.

"Would ya mind giving Dominick a call?" The vamp whimpers at his king's name. "Let him know we've got a misbehaving vamp for him to pick up."

By the time I've finished my sentence, Billy already has his phone out and up to his ear. He takes a couple of seconds to relay my message before hanging up and sliding the phone into his back pocket.

"There are a couple of wolves outside who I'm going to send home. Then I'll show Dominick in when he arrives. Are you okay with him?" He nods towards the vampire who's still holding his head in his hands.

I wipe my nose with the back of my hand and see the blood as I lift my arm away. Magic always takes a toll, and it usually demands payment in blood or power.

"We'll be fine." I give my wrist a sudden flick, effectively breaking the vamp's neck.

The vampire's body slumps to the floor and Billy gives me an appraising look. "Jesus, sugar." He clears his throat. "I need to get some air before I do something to embarrass myself," he says, walking back out the door. I catch sight of him adjusting himself in his pants before the door closes and I realise what he meant with his parting words. Could seeing me snapping a neck really have turned him on? Werewolves are known for being violent. I guess that could float his boat.

I step over the vamp as I go about cleaning the bar. He isn't dead, just incapacitated until his body heals. I'm sure Dominick will be here to deal with him long before he comes to.

There are only a couple of ways to kill a vampire: staking and beheading. Not everyone knows that there are a few other tricks, like the one I just shared with Billy. Dominick will probably be pissed at me for that, but I'll deal with those consequences later.

I slam the dishwasher closed and stand up to find Billy and Dominick strolling in the front door. They're like polar opposites. Dominick is tall, dark, and handsome, always impeccable in a suit with his wiry frame and dark curls hanging around his face, whereas Billy looks rough and dangerous in his jeans and biker leathers, with his shaved head and large muscular body.

I shake my head as I rake my eyes over their bodies, trying to kill the thoughts of having them in my bed. *Jesus!* I'd sworn I would never date another supernatural creature. Not after my ex. He was an angel, except he acted more like a demon. He was so controlling and, after seeing how the werewolves act around their mates, I can only imagine Billy would be the same. Not to mention Dominick; he likes to control anything that breathes in his territory. The alpha of the Mount Roxby pack, Theo, has had to push for equal pegging in their joint ownership of the area.

"Like something you see?" Billy smirks, catching me ogling.

Dominick straightens the cuffs of his jacket. "She was clearly looking at me. This suit is fitted to perfection, after all."

I roll my eyes. "I was deciding, if I took ya both to bed with me, who'd bottom for who?" I say with a smirk. It wasn't exactly a lie. The question *had* crossed my mind when I pictured them naked in my bed.

It's well known that Dominick doesn't care about gender when he chooses his lovers. His ex-boyfriend recently turned up and caused havoc in the town. Not only did his actions make Dominick sire the alpha's sister, turning her into a vampire, but he also murdered Theo's beta wolf, his second. He did it all as a punishment because Dominick wouldn't make him a vampire, so I'm not surprised to see Dominick step aside and give Billy a thorough eyeing from head to foot.

"I don't bottom for anyone, but I'd definitely be happy to..." He raises a brow and a smirk crosses his face. "...*wrestle* with him over the position."

Billy steps up close so their chests are touching. "For me you will." He places a kiss on Dominick's lips, biting his bottom lip between his teeth before pulling away. "And you'll be begging to do it again." My mouth goes dry at the sight before me. *Holy shit.* I blink, unable to believe what I'm seeing.

The groans of the vamp at my feet break the heated moment.

"Bitch!" he calls as he grips my ankles, digging his nails in and drawing blood. His fangs descend at the smell of my blood, but I don't worry about him trying to feed from me. My wards won't allow such severe violence in the building. Well, unless

I'm the one inflicting the violence. Dominick suddenly appears on this side of the bar, dragging the vampire up by his throat. He apparently doesn't care about the pain my wards are causing him. I throw out a hand and mutter a few words, disabling them.

"That wasn't necessary, but thank you." He walks around the bar, pausing as he reaches the door. "This—" He points his finger between Billy, me, and back to himself. "—we'll deal with this another night when the sun isn't so close to rising." He smiles. "I have a feeling we'll need plenty of time to explore things thoroughly." He disappears out the door, and I struggle to tear my eyes away from the purple painted wood.

Billy clears his throat and I watch him lock the door. "Well, that was… interesting."

I laugh. "That's not the word I'd use to describe it." I take a deep, calming breath and pull my shoulder-length hair back into a loose ponytail with an elastic band I always keep around my wrist. "Jesus, I never would've guessed ya swung that way. It was just a fantasy that popped into my head and I couldn't keep my damn mouth shut," I say while walking around the bar and straightening the stools.

I feel Billy step up behind me. "Have I ever told you how much I like your British accent?" Placing a hand on my hip, he spins me around before sliding his other hand over my shoulder and around my neck. I grip his biceps and shake my head. "Dominick intrigues me. Someone needs to take his control away, and I wouldn't mind that being me."

He crushes his lips against mine, as if he's trying to prove he doesn't only like guys. "I'd certainly swing for you, sugar," he says, brushing his lips against mine before capturing them in another kiss. I slide my hands up his arms and around his neck as I lose myself in the moment.

ACKNOWLEDGEMENTS

I want to thank *my family* for supporting me unconditionally. I love you all to pieces.

Marisa from Cover Me darling LLC, thank you for coming up with this amazing cover. I love your designs and can't wait to work on more books with you.

Becky from Hot Tree Editing, you really made me work hard to get this story to be what it is today and I thank you with my whole heart.

Hot Tree Editing Beta Team, Thank you for your input. It was fantastic to have those extra sets of eyes.

Sam Destiny, My Parabatai, where do I start? You are my rock. Thank you for being there for me on a daily basis. Whenever I'm feeling low, you are right there from across the world sending me your support. We mustn't forget those amazing gifs and your fabulous stories that keep me smiling everyday. Love ya, girl.

Claire, I love your chapter headers thank you so much for doing them for me.

Finally, I'd like to thank you guys, the readers. Your support and love for my books mean everything to me. I love my stories and characters but knowing that you guys love them too means the world to me. Thank YOU.

ABOUT THE AUTHOR

Aimie is a Yorkshire lass calling Queensland, Australia, home. She is a mother to three boys.

Aimie loves to people watch, it's her favourite way to come up with new characters and stories. So next time a stranger is staring at you in the street don't panic, they could be an author basing a character on you.

Aimie has always loved to read and write. Her favourite place to listen to her characters is at the beach.

Aimie would love to hear from you. Comments and questions are always welcome.

For more information:
www.aimiejennison.com
aimiejennison@gmail.com

ALSO BY
AIMIE JENNISON

Mount Roxby Series

Pride to Pack

Forever Young and Beautiful

Rossi Pack Series

Releasing the Wolf